CURRENTS

TURNER PUBLISHING COMPANY
Nashville, Tennessee
www.turnerpublishing.com

CURRENTS
Copyright © 2020 Jeremy Scott
All rights reserved

This is a work of fiction. All the characters and events portrayed in this book are either products of the author's imagination or are used fictitiously.

Cover design: Callie Lawson
Book design: Karen Sheets de Gracia

Library of Congress Cataloging-in-Publication Data Upon Request

9781684423439 Hardcover
9781684423422 Paperback
9781684423446 eBook

PRINTED IN THE UNITED STATES OF AMERICA
20 21 22 23 24   10 9 8 7 6 5 4 3 2 1

CURRENTS

THE ABLES ⚡ BOOK THREE

JEREMY SCOTT

TURNER

PUBLISHING COMPANY

This book is dedicated to anyone who ever had their path decided for them; to anyone overlooked, underestimated, or simply passed over; to anyone whose aspirations rise above limitations; and to all those who choose to step out of their own comfort to aid or assist another. You're all heroes.

THE RIVER

The forest was like a song to me.

The deep hum of the nearby river provided the base line. The crackling fire the percussion. The soft breeze was a cello.

The voices of my friends made up the choir, their laughter dancing like a melody.

The crickets and owls and other forest sounds filled in as background singers, countermelodies, and record scratches.

I never got tired of this song.

We were back in upstate New York for our annual camping trip. It had become a tradition almost before the first trip had finished. Bentley's family had some land on the US side of the Saint Lawrence River—which was a massive body of water flowing between Lake Ontario and . . . well, basically the Atlantic Ocean. We always came out for the last weekend before school started.

Of course, the group had grown and shifted over the years.

The core members were all back this year. That meant Bentley and Penelope, now engaged to be married. Emmaline and I were here, as well as Patrick, Freddie, and Greta.

We were joined this year by newcomers Lacene and Luc, fraternal twins who we'd met and bonded with during our freshman year at Goodspeed University. They were from France, but their English was perfect. They did enjoy speaking privately to each other in French so we wouldn't know what they were saying. It was annoying. Fortunately, they were charming and quite funny.

Lacene was a telepath, like Henry had been, though her ability was not as strong as his. Despite several attempts, she'd never been able to send me an image the way Henry had. I didn't hold it against her; Henry had ultimately proved to be far more powerful than any of us had realized . . . even him.

Luc was an EMP, an electromagnetic pulse generator, and he was the kind of guy that would let you know about it immediately, then remind you about it a few minutes later. Cocky, overconfident, and self-centered—we all loved him.

The final new addition to this year's group was Echo. Echo was mute. Apparently she'd been able to speak just fine until her eighth birthday, when she was in a terrible car accident; she had been unbuckled.

Echo communicated via sign language or sometimes using an electronic text-to-speech device. Despite her lack of a voice, she had one of the most effusive personalities I'd ever encountered. Her starting setting was Bubbly Fun and it only went up from there.

Echo was a kinesthetic, meaning she learned about objects and people through the sense of touch. She could grab your shoulder and tell your momma things that would make you blush.

"I can't believe we have to get up early tomorrow and drive," Patrick sighed.

"Some people have never been to New York City and would like to do some sightseeing." I squeezed Emm's hand. "You are not obligated to join us."

"But even if you want to sightsee—she's a teleporter, Phillip! Just . . . zap there and have more time for sightseeing!"

It's hard for a nonteleporter to understand the joy those with the ability can take in a traditional journey. It's something I myself was still trying to comprehend. But I'd gotten to a point where it at least made sense to me from a logical standpoint. A teleporter can zap anywhere in a second, so they often do, which means rides on trains or cars or planes are new or rare experiences for them. It's weird how sometimes the people that value their time the most seem to be wasting it to the untrained eyes of the people who value time the least.

"The drive is part of the fun, Patty." My girlfriend was literally the only person in the world who could get away with calling my brother Patty. She just had a way of saying it that was so . . . familiar and kind. Patrick never once objected.

It was a different story for me, even though that didn't stop me. "Yeah, Patty, the drive is part of the—"

Before I could finish, Patrick raced over and rapid-punched my left arm a dozen times before racing back to his seat. Though it was likely no one saw more than a blur, the pain in my arm and the slight shift of the fire's heat told me it had been real.

Everyone laughed because they knew what Patrick had done even if they hadn't quite seen it, because this was only the 105th time we'd done this routine.

I'd found that a lot of what makes family family revolves around routines. Scripts. No conditions, just unwritten instructions everyone inherently knows.

"So what is everyone planning to see in New York?" Lacene asked.

I turned toward Echo. I always wondered if she ever wanted to go first. She never tried to—not that I would've seen it anyway. Blind from birth, I had not been able to see anything since the death of Henry, whose powers had allowed me a kind of sight for my first few years as a custodian.

"I'm going to a Yankees game," Freddie blurted, unable to contain his excitement. He'd been to the Big Apple a few times before but had never seen his favorite baseball team play in person.

"Aren't they terrible this year?" Luc cracked.

"Yes!" Freddie responded with no less enthusiasm.

Greta was next. "I wanna see some art!" She was more excited about art than Freddie was about baseball, and it startled me a bit. But she also got Echo to perk up and communicate that she wanted to join that excursion if Greta didn't mind. And Greta didn't mind. Greta was the most agreeable person I'd ever met.

"I think we're doing more of a monument kind of thing," I said, instinctively turning to Emm to clarify.

"Statue of Liberty," she began, to groans all around. "Statue of Liberty," she repeated defiantly. "Central Park—"

"That's not a monument," Luc joked.

She ignored him. "And the Freedom Tower and the 9/11 Memorial & Museum."

Emmaline had never spent more than a few seconds in New York City, and she was more than ready to make up for it.

"Bentley?" I asked.

"We're going to see one of the shows on Broadway."

A Broadway show was typical Bentley and Penelope. I smiled at their plans.

"How about you, Pat? Where are you headed?" Patrick was about to turn nineteen and start his first year of university. I had to constantly remind myself how close in age we were, because my brain just filed him long ago as "little brother" and was struggling to adapt to the fact that he was now also a fellow college student.

"FOOOOOOOOD!" he shouted. "I'm going to Brooklyn for pizza for lunch, then to midtown for a sushi spot I heard was top-notch, then to Times Square for some fine-dining dinner!"

"By yourself?" I knew Patrick didn't care, but I was still surprised he didn't want company.

"I'll take Sherpa," he teased.

"False," I objected. Everyone knew that Sherpa was "my" dog, in that she was literally a service dog that helped my blind ass get around without too much trouble. She loved Patrick, and she protected him too, but she was my canine soul mate, and Pat knew it.

"Fine. I figure I'll meet a girl somewhere along the way, anyway." I could hear his smarmy smile in the tenor of his words.

"Ew," Emmaline replied, for all of us.

"Frenchies?" We'd all taken to referring to Luc and Lacene collectively as the "Frenchies." They said it was funny, so we didn't feel wrong about it. And it was just easier to lump them together since they were so inseparable in general.

They responded to my question by speaking to each other in French.

"Combien voulez-vous leur dire?" Lacene said quickly.

"Rien," Luc replied.

"Combien de temps devons-nous porter ce secret?"

"Aussi longtemps qu'il faudra."

They stopped after that.

"You guys done? Did you work out where you want to go?" I asked.

After a few seconds of silence, Luc finally spoke. "We will go to Coney Island."

"What?" Patrick bellowed. "You'll spend most of the day on the trains!"

"Coney Island," Lacene repeated. "Coney Island."

Whatever. It's a free day for everyone. Let them do what they want, I told myself.

"Well," I said with great inflection, "we've all got some driving and a big day of sightseeing ahead of us. Perhaps we should kill the fire and head off to bed?"

"I think you're forgetting one very important part of the annual camping trip," Freddie said, giggling.

And only just then did I remember—the pledge. Somehow I managed to forget about the pledge every single year until right at the end.

Everyone stood and put both hands on their hips. For the most part, I faked or whispered my way through the chant, because I was tired, and because I had come to stop believing in its words.

"I am," the chant began. "I am here on this Earth." I felt Emm squeeze my hand, as she knew my struggle with this particular ritual of our culture.

The chant was created after the showdown on the Mall of Washington. As a way to define our own voice, and let humans know we were on their side, some custodian with a flair for words wrote up a pledge. We said it in school. We said it in our homes. We bought commercial airtime on national networks and hired real actors to do the pledge so the viewers would begin to fear us less.

To me it was just empty words. We could tell people we mean well over and over and over, but words are only words; actions were how one showed his or her true merit as a human or custodian.

I hated the chant.

"I have been given special abilities for a reason, and I will not turn my back on that responsibility. To whatever extent I have been made extra, I pledge to give extra of myself to my fellow men and women. I vow to give my all to . . ."

The words slowly faded off and dissipated as I turned my mind from this moment to a set of memories I often revisited. Deep inside my brain was the memory of Henry's suicide, which I had decided had only been necessary due to my own weakness.

I'd been too weak to kill Henry myself, and had thereby forced his hand. For that, I would never forgive myself. But even beyond that, I had been too weak, from a superhero standpoint, to actually do what he'd asked. My friend who couldn't walk had ten times the backbone I would ever have.

Most evenings I awoke several times from nightmares . . . all related to that moment. How I could have played it differently. How I might have tried to save him if I'd known what was coming.

First James and now Henry. I was growing weary of killing my friends. My therapist said it was a fixation. I thought it was just a reality. I'd killed two of my friends by being a jerk. I saw no need to sugarcoat it.

The silver lining was that my PTSD from Henry's death had at least erased my PTSD from the Finch encounter—or replaced it, I guess, to be more honest. Look, if anyone's allowed to joke about my mental health, it's me.

"This is my vow," said everyone but me. It jolted me out of my daydream. "Vow," I said, too late and obviously so.

Typically Emm would take my hand and lead the way back to our tent, guiding me around the logs and other obstructions. Tonight, I think she knew I was close to a panic attack, so she just zapped us back instantly.

Ooph!

I let out a huge sigh.

"It's not doing you any good to keep dwelling on it, P." I had shortened her name from Emmaline to Emm, but she'd shortened mine from Phillip to just P. As usual, no one was about to argue with her.

"I know," I agreed. "I'm not sure I can help it."

Sherpa, who had not been teleported, caught up to us and sauntered into the tent, settling between the two of us and hoping for tummy rubs.

"What does your therapist say about it?"

"She tells me to exercise more and to do meditation."

"And?"

"I exercise plenty."

Emm expelled air so quickly you could almost call it spitting.

"Meditation doesn't work for me," I offered, knowing it was an argument that would get demolished.

"You don't try *enough*," she spat back, correctly.

"Emm," I said softly, "I don't want to keep having this fight."

"Then *change!*" She was done. She rolled over and wouldn't speak to me again for ten hours. I always knew when she was done, and it was usually frustrating because it meant she was right—and I was wrong.

I started rubbing the dog's stomach. Sherpa was extremely protective of me, and she'd typically get between me and anyone who raised their voice to me. Except Emm. Those two had some weird understanding.

I knew my current path was ill-advised. I knew I needed to change course. I just wasn't sure how.

As usual, I struggled to fall asleep. I lay there kicking the same thoughts around my head.

I missed Henry.

I missed having sight. I missed the sight my friend allowed me to have, and I felt guilty for missing it. I'd never done anything to earn it, and I had largely taken it for granted. And now I was blind again.

I knew Emmaline was one of the best things to ever happen to me and that I was in danger of losing her because the work to improve my mental health seemed too hard. Maybe I was just being lazy.

When I did sleep, I dreamed of Henry and me on a raft. He was standing, no wheelchair in sight, as he watched the waters of the river before us.

"Where are we going?" I asked loudly into the night air.

Henry smiled. "Wherever it takes us, of course." He pointed ahead.

"Don't we have any control?" I yelled back.

"I have none. You have less." He suddenly kicked me into the water.

I awoke with a gasp and a sweat-soaked sleeping bag. It was sixty degrees out here, but just like when I was sleeping at home, I was a sweaty, panicky mess.

2

ROAD TRIP

To hear my friends tell it, the drive from upstate New York to New York City is one of the most gorgeous drives a human can take. I listened to them ooh and aah for hours, smiling for them.

I'd be lying if I said I didn't also want to see the beautiful terrain. I was definitely still happy for my friends' ability to enjoy the countryside. I tried to view my few years of vision-via-Henry as a gift, an unexpected bonus. And there was talk the science guys in Goodspeed were making solid progress on technology that could help me see for real one day in the future.

I tried to be content just to be alive. To have friends. To still be able to make some kind of difference in this world.

The drive to the city was shorter than I had expected, but time is relative, so I may have just gotten lost in some daydreams. But regardless, before I knew it, we were crossing the George Washington Bridge. We'd left early, at six o'clock, so we were arriving just after lunchtime. Plenty of time for all our varied agendas.

"Remember," I said, probably in a nagging tone I didn't intend, "we meet back at eleven tonight at Bryant Park—just near Times Square and adjacent to the New York Public Library. Then we all zap back home via Emmaline. Cool?"

Various replies came back, all affirmative: "Cool." "Got it." "Yep."

"Everyone have fun." I actually meant it.

When everyone had gone their own way, Emmaline finally started talking to me.

"What was your dream about?"

"What?"

She sighed. "You were screaming and then you sat up panting and gasping for air."

"You noticed that?"

"How could I not? Listen, Phil, I care about you too much to ignore what's going on with you. I know you are dealing with things outside your control, I know there's grief and guilt and pain . . . but I need you to let me in. We've had a good few years, but I am not signing up for a lifetime of being left in the dark."

"It's Henry," I said as we walked toward a taxi-heavy intersection.

She said nothing, giving me the chance to go at my own pace.

"I should have been the one to do it."

"You think you should have killed him?" Her voice was a perfect mix of confusion and love.

"I think he shouldn't have had to do it himself." I broke down, slumping onto the sidewalk, tears forming instantly.

"Okay, okay," she said, dragging me to a nearby staircase, though Sherpa was already doing the same thing, as she'd been trained to intervene if I showed signs of distress.

"You think the taxis will ignore us as long as I'm crying?"

"I do, yes," she said honestly. "But I'm not concerned about taxis right now. Let's talk about this Henry thing."

Instead of talking about it, I just cried for twenty minutes. Emm was a saint; she comforted me and never pushed the discussion further. Eventually I calmed down and made a joke about how many tissues I'd personally been responsible for soiling. She laughed, and we were back on our way to the Statue of Liberty.

Emmaline was a hopeless romantic, at least with regard to tourism. She loved seeing the sights, the more cliché the better.

She was giddy all the way out to Liberty Island, up the Statue of Liberty, and back to Manhattan Island.

She didn't complain about the cost, which was higher than expected. She didn't complain about the smell on the ferry, which was litigious. She didn't complain about the time spent waiting in line, which was substantial. She wanted to see the Statue of Liberty and she did, and nothing else mattered. Honestly her enthusiasm was one of her most attractive qualities. She was, in a great many ways, what I endeavored to be.

After Liberty Island, we headed for the financial district and the 9/11 monuments.

We were both too young when the 9/11 attacks took place to remember the actual events, but we'd been taught about them in school, where they had shown the videos and documentaries time and time again.

The 9/11 Memorial consists of two infinity fountains—where the water appears to fall forever—in the exact location and dimensions of the original twin towers.

Emm told me she spotted a worker going around adding flowers to some of the names etched into the marble memorial wall.

"What do the flowers mean?" she inquired.

"We put a flower on the name whenever it's their birthday," the worker responded.

"There are so many . . ." Emmaline said. Hearing that there were that many birthdays just reminded me of the overall number of lives lost.

It's sobering stuff. Emm clutched my hand harder than ever before as we stood in relative silence with thousands of other visitors. Even Sherpa was quiet—though she was usually quiet.

"This is the kind of thing we're supposed to prevent," Emmaline said under her breath, almost to herself.

"I'm not sure anyone could have prevented this," I said honestly. Custodians had superpowers, sure, but they didn't have high-level intelligence reports.

"You ready to go up?" She said this knowing full well I would never be ready to go up a hundred-story-plus building. Still, I had promised, so I nodded.

You may be wondering how a blind person could be afraid of heights. But fear of heights, fear of falling—these things are not as based on sight as people tend to think. In fact, the hearing and inner ear function is more likely to drive a fear of heights than anything based on sight. And the mind is also very powerful. If I simply know I'm on the hundredth floor of a building, I don't need to see it to get weak in the knees.

Of course, all fears come down to a fear of death. It all revolves around the fear that one will cease to exist and therefore lose all chance to ever leave a legacy or leave a mark or leave a whisper.

The elevator ride up Freedom Tower is something special. The walls are all televisions, and as you ascend you see a rapid time-lapse of New York City growing and changing around you over the years—well, sighted people see it. There's even a moment Emm called "breathtaking" when the twin towers go up as they are built and then a few seconds later in the time-lapse . . . disappear.

Finally, at the top, the screens drop and reveal windows showcasing the near entirety of Manhattan Island.

Based on the time, I knew the sun had nearly dropped behind the horizon and the lights of New York had probably begun to glimmer and shine. Again I wished for sight.

Then there was a faint popping noise, a quick silence, followed by total chaos.

The hundred or so fellow tourists behind me gasped, talked, and a few even screamed.

"Power went out," Emm whispered, trying to keep me in the loop.

"Here or everywhere?" I asked. The answer would be important.

"Everywhere," she answered. "There isn't any sign of electricity as far as the eye can see."

"But the windows . . . You can still—"

"I can still see through the windows. But the only light is moonlight and its reflections."

I tapped my earpiece. "Bentley, are you there? Can you hear me?" There was no response. The radios would need to make use of Wi-Fi, and Wi-Fi was probably down.

"Ladies and gentlemen, please do not panic," said a college-aged employee whose voice suggested he himself was already panicking. "We have experts looking into it."

Experts? I thought. *Freedom Tower employs multiple experts in the area of citywide power outages?*

"The power went out in the whole city!" came a voice behind me.

"What's happening?" cried another.

"Are we dead?"

"Is it aliens?"

I began to think I'd joined the most conspiracy-theory-minded group tour of all time.

Suddenly I heard the sound of an explosion. My fellow tour takers erupted in another round of screams. Emm told me that all anyone saw from the top floor was a massive fireball. We reasoned many died in the explosion.

"Oh no," exclaimed a woman behind me as she started sobbing.

"We have to . . . we have to help," said a man who sounded twenty years too old to help.

"We can't sit up here and do nothing," I said, mostly to Emmaline, though I'm sure everyone else heard as well.

"I agree," she replied.

"Are you kids high?" The voice came from the group standing behind us. We both turned our heads to find the speaker. "The elevators are dead, like all the other electrical systems in the city. And it'll take you an hour just to run down those stairs. So how do you get around that?"

I smiled wide, grabbed Emm's hand and Sherpa's collar, and replied, "By cheating."

Ooph!

Emm and I disappeared, leaving behind an entire tour group of what I hoped were highly confused patrons.

Westfield World Trade Center was a blend of shopping and transportation. Entirely underground—though with a sliver of an open roof running across the top—it was essentially a very sleek and modern shopping mall. It had several levels, all with views of the main concourse. That concourse led to another level that was a humongous subway station.

There's a certain amount of genius involved in placing a multistory shopping mall between a subway station and the street level above. This place was probably minting money.

But right now it was on fire, and what used to be a sliver of roof was now a gaping hole.

Emmaline had teleported us onto the main concourse. From what she could ascertain, an explosion had occurred on the second level, just above us. A hundred-foot section was charred and in flames. There was damage on the third floor above the explosion, and plenty of damage here on the concourse due to debris and falling sections of stone and metal.

"This is chaos," I breathed.

I couldn't triage the situation and find the most important thing to address without sight. "What's the biggest issue you can see?" I asked her.

"Fire. Lots of fire. Lots of injured, but we aren't EMTs."

"Is there an exit for people?"

"I think so. I see a bunch running. Hang on."

Ooph!

I usually hated when she teleported away midconversation, but this time I figured it was understandable.

Ooph!

"Yep. Clear path from this concourse to the main staircase up to the street level."

"Alright," I said, wheels turning. "So we need to put out fires. Who do we know that could help us put out fires?" I asked like some kind of weird midcrisis game show host.

There was a sudden whooshing noise and a burst of wind. "Hey, guys." It was Patrick.

"Patrick?" Emm exclaimed in wonder.

"No, not Patrick—Penelope!" I shouted, almost annoyed that Pat had interrupted me by showing up just now.

"How did you know where to find us?" Emmaline asked, shocked.

"Power outage, I knew you were at the tower thingy . . . saw the fire, figured you had too . . . bing bang boom. Here I am." He made it all sound so rational.

"Here he is!" I cackled madly.

"I can't put out fires, though," Patrick added. "I'm actually bad with fire. I can only run fast and make a light wind, and wind makes fire grow faster."

"Thank you for the science lesson," I said sarcastically.

"We need Penelope," Emm stated, realizing I was right.

I agreed. "The radios aren't going to work without power because they require internet. We're going to have to go old school to find her."

"We don't have to find her," Patrick said cheerily. "They went to see the revival of *Les Misèrables*." We didn't react, so he continued. "On Broadway. It's playing in only one theater, guys—the Tanger."

"Okay, okay," I said, finally formulating a plan. "Emm, you go to the Tanger, find Penelope and Bent, and zap them here to help with the fire. Pat, we know that Greta and Echo were going to look at various art institutions . . . could be anywhere. But we know for certain Freddie is at the Yankees game. You go find Freddie and race him back here as fast as you can. Got it?"

Emmaline had some concerns. "So you're just going to stand here, while people run around and the building burns, waiting for us to come back with reinforcements?"

"I have Sherpa. And it's only going to take seconds. You guys have powers that work very quickly. In fact, challenge Patrick to a race to see who gets back here faster and see how quickly he moves."

"Deal," Patrick said, before tearing off at full speed. He was probably halfway to Yankee Stadium before I took my next breath.

Emm sighed. "You stay here and don't move."

"Yes, ma'am."

Ooph!

What none of us knew in that moment was that Penelope and Bentley had changed their minds last minute and had gone to see *Cats* instead of *Les Mis*.

Or that Freddie had been so enthusiastic about being at the Yankees game that he'd fallen over the rail onto the field and had been arrested and placed in the stadium lockup for "jumping" onto the field during the game.

Or that I was about to hear the very urgent cries of some subway riders trapped one hundred yards down the tube from the Westfield platform.

3

GUESSES

READER NOTE: *This chapter contains visual elements of events our first-person narrator, Phillip, was not present for, which were relayed to him after the fact by his friends.*

I didn't expect to be standing alone waiting for very long. Emmaline's power was instantaneous; she'd show up in a blacked-out theater, call out for Bentley and Penelope, navigate to them, and zap back. I thought it would take maybe thirty seconds.

I gave Patrick even odds. He'd zip up to Yankee Stadium, grab Freddie, and maybe be back even before Emm. Patrick was fast . . . like really fast. And he probably hadn't even reached his full potential yet. Lately when we'd "raced" to answer the phone, his speed beat out my telekinesis most but not all of the time.

Thirty seconds came and went. Then sixty. Then ninety.

"Sherp," I said to my dog, "I don't think I like this."

Eventually I realized things had gone wrong. But I couldn't go after Pat or Emmaline, because I was a blind guy. I could try telekinetically flying, but I'd certainly hit a ceiling or wall or building and injure myself.

No, I was stuck here. I had to trust my brother and girlfriend to manage their own crises. I would stay here and do whatever I could to help.

So . . . what could I do to help?

To my left, I heard people continuing to run by and up the stairs to the street. I could hear fire extinguishers going off above me, presumably putting out the source of the blaze.

But to my right, and quite faintly, I heard a guttural, urgent cry. Something in my subconscious recognized the pain in that cry and understood it.

I grabbed the bannister near me and began walking slowly down the stairs toward the subway platform, toward that sound. Sherpa darted in front of me to lead the way.

My hearing was elevated above a normal person's, and no one seemed to hear the cries but me. All the bodies I passed were moving rapidly in the other direction.

One of them was moving so quickly he kicked out my left foot, and I tumbled down the last three steps to the marble floor below.

"Oh," I moaned.

That's gonna leave several marks.

"Sorry, man!" I heard some asshole yell from halfway up the stairs.

You can shove your sorry in a sack, I thought.

Having made sure I was okay, Sherpa turned and gave the guy a good bark.

"You tell him, girl."

The cries grew louder and more urgent. They were coming from my right side. I gathered myself together, stood up, and pulled out my clicker.

While I was no dolphin, I had begun to dabble a bit more in a crude form of echolocation. Bentley had created this small button that fit on my key ring. He called it the clicker. Whenever I pushed it, a clicking noise rang out from my position and then echoed back at me from various locations in front of and all around me.

It was a way of getting a feel for the landscape. It wasn't as precise as real vision, but it was enough to let me move around a bit on my own.

Thirteen miles north, Patrick arrived at Yankee Stadium.

They had already begun evacuation procedures, and battery-operated emergency lights had kicked on, so there was a little bit of light.

But it was not bright enough for Patrick to find Freddie in a sea of twenty thousand fans.

So he did what any annoying little brother would have done in the same situation: he started yelling "Freddie" as loud as he could, over and over.

⚡

Lacene and Luc had always wanted to visit Coney Island. They wanted the full experience. So first they went for an authentic hot dog, which both found rather disgusting. Next they both ate cotton candy, which again they found disgusting. But they were still having fun doing a clichéd American experience.

They got on the Ferris wheel, hoping for some great views. And the greatest view came at the very top of the Ferris wheel's circle, looking back at Manhattan's lights.

Unfortunately, that's also when the power went out all around them, as far as they could see.

"Zut alor, Luc, what did you do?" Lacene sighed.

"Nothing! This wasn't me!" Luc declared. You couldn't really blame Lacene for asking, since Luc's EMP powers were more often than not the cause for the localized power outages that she had experienced firsthand.

"Seriously?"

"Seriously."

"Then what was it?" She sounded a little frightened now.

"I don't know. But it looks like more than one grid is affected."

⚡

Emmaline popped into the Tanger theater, which had been playing *Les Mis* until the blackout. She instantly started calling out for Bentley and Penelope, unaware they were across the street in a competing theater's audience for *Cats*.

"Bentley!"

"I'll take a Bentley home," replied a clueless and slightly drunk rich person. "I didn't know they had Bentley taxis," he gushed.

"That's hilarious," Emm replied flatly.

Ooph!

⚡

Using the clicker, I got down all the steps to the main subway platform and followed the wall down to the actual track ledge.

"Help! She's having a baby! Help!" I was close enough now to make out the words and thereby understand the urgency in the cries.

"I'm coming!" I bellowed without thinking. I didn't know how far away they were, and I certainly didn't know how to deliver a baby or how to quickly move a pregnant woman.

And how was I going to get down the tunnel to help?

⚡

"Freddie!" Patrick yelled for the twelfth time. "Fredddddieeee!"

Eventually the audience members in line to be evacuated got bored and started yelling "Freddie" as well. Maybe they were drunk. Maybe they were just looking for a distraction from the blackout and ongoing evacuation.

The call and answer between Pat and the lingering fans grew to a chant significant in its decibel range. He would call out "Freddie!" A second would pass, then fifteen thousand voices would yell out "Freddie!"

Suddenly there was a minor earthquake, and the entire stadium started rumbling.

⚡

"Penelope!"

Emmaline was now in her third Broadway theater yelling out Bentley's and Penelope's names. They hadn't been in *Les Misèrables* as they had planned.

They hadn't been in *Hamilton*, *Moana*, or *Phantom*. Emm was beginning to wonder if they'd ended up seeing *any* Broadway show.

They could be anywhere, she thought. *I can't waste too much time on this. I hope Phil's okay.*

$\lightning$

Lacene employed her telepathy and eventually realized that no one really knew what was going on except that a massive blackout had hit the entirety of NYC and all surrounding areas, including Coney Island.

Telepathy had distance limits, though they were different for every telepath.

So with her stunted telepathy and Luc's EMP power . . . they were every bit as stuck in their current car as every other Ferris wheel rider.

"We have to get down from here," Lacene said.

"Okay," Luc agreed tentatively. "But how?"

Lacene looked down again and then directly into her twin brother's eyes. "We climb."

$\lightning$

The ground beneath Yankee Stadium shook violently. Near the second base marker, the earth began to give way and turn to dust. Soon a large head appeared in the opening, and then a giant torso rose through the infield and shook off the debris.

"Yawwwwwwww!" Patrick heard a loud sustained scream that was primal and guttural.

Freddie, now four stories tall, had just broken through from the underground stadium holding cell for drunks and other game arrestees and up onto the field itself.

"Freddie!" Pat shouted from the upper deck.

The giant Freddie, still shaking off dirt, turned and waved at Pat.

The fans evacuating the stadium all started running, as though they'd never seen any supernatural shit before, when they definitely had.

⚡

Inching around the corner of the subway platform and tapping with my cane, I finally found a narrow staircase that seemed to lead down into the tunnel itself.

I turned to my dog. "Sherpa, stay." It was the toughest command for her to follow because it meant she wouldn't be leading me and protecting me, which she viewed as her life's mission. Whenever I told her to stay, she whimpered a bit, but she always stayed right where she was.

I continued using both my cane and the clicker to make my way down the stairs and then was delighted to find a narrow utility walkway—maybe eight inches wide. The cries for help were coming from a subway car farther down the track, so I shuffled along the grated metal walkway. I could tell I was getting much closer.

I was nearly on top of them when the service walkway ended.

"Help us!" a man yelled from the rear platform of the train.

He sounded pretty close. "How much distance between us?" I asked.

He was silent a moment, probably eyeballing it. "About six feet."

He sounds pretty confident, I thought. *And if I try climbing down and walking across the track, I'm definitely going to trip.*

"Back up," I barked. And then I jumped.

⚡

"Penelope!"

Emmaline had been moving in a fairly logical pattern. They had planned on seeing *Les Mis* but were musical fans in general, so it made sense they'd be in another musical's audience. So Emm had gone with the most popular and best reviewed shows, working her way down the list.

Now she was running out of theaters to even check, and she was pretty certain they weren't going to be in this one.

"Emmaline?" came a faint reply, in the form of a question. "Is that you?"

There was a three-second pause.

"You went to *Cats?*" Emm bellowed, incredulous.

Bentley stammered before offering, "*Les Mis* was sold out."

"If you had better taste, I would have found you ages ago!"

⚡

The Ferris wheel had a ladder from the center of the wheel down to the ground. The twins only needed to climb down to that center point, and they were nearly there. Both were athletic and strong.

"This would be a lot easier if there wasn't the constant fear of death," Luc said and laughed.

"Let's just get down and see what we can do," his sister replied. "Your jokes aren't helping."

"If I thought my jokes were helping, there would be no point in telling them." He grinned. No one thought Luc was funnier than Luc did.

⚡

Before me on the train car was a pregnant woman, so I was told. She smelled sweaty and clammy, and she was screaming her face off. I knew immediately that I was in over my head.

There have to be EMTs and emergency personnel showing up here by now, right? I asked myself. *Is that just wishful thinking? Do I even have any other options? I can't do this myself, can I?*

I didn't have a lot of choices. Clearly no one on this subway car could help deliver a baby or they would have stepped forward already. I couldn't do it personally. I had to hope someone back at the Westfield World Trade Center mall would be able to help.

"Are . . . are you blind?" a stranger asked. I ignored them.

I listened around the very full subway car, clicking and relistening, did some quick math in my head, and then went to the rear of the car again and jumped from the back of the train toward the service walkway.

As I disappeared I heard the riders groan and gasp, thinking I was abandoning them.

My landing was less than perfect, as my shoe nicked a handrail on the metal walkway and I tumbled into a ball.

No one's going to hear about this part of the evening, I told myself. I climbed to my feet and moved rapidly.

My memory was pretty good. If I was going to brag about something, it would be my ability to retrace steps or be ultracomfortable and mobile in any place I had been before. I was jogging, then running on the metal grate until I lifted off and actually just flew back to the subway platform.

There was no time to waste. I shook off my jacket and stretched both arms out over the tracks back down the tunnel, palms turned toward the car with the pregnant woman on board.

I felt around with my telekinesis for a bit; I needed at least a *decent* grip to move an object this large. Finally I found two spots I liked and grabbed hold of my target. Now all that was left was the toughest part.

I pulled with my mind. I meditated even while I deployed my brain's full power. *Calm to get strong. Peace to bring war. Love to deliver pain.* I didn't know that I believed any of it. I'd picked it up from a martial arts book when I was younger. It wasn't the meaning of the words that was the point, it was the ritual of preparing my mind for conflict and boosting my self-confidence.

The scraping sound of metal on metal got louder the more momentum I built, and the car began to slide along the tracks under my control.

"Okay, that was awesome," Patrick admitted while standing just beyond second base in Yankee Stadium. Or . . . what had recently been second base.

"Thanks," giant Freddie said, kind of impressed with himself.

"Can you get small again? I need to get us both back down to Freedom Tower ASAP."

"It takes about ten minutes, man. I'm sorry," Freddie replied.

"Crap!"

"Unless you have some caffeine. That seems to speed things—"

Before he could finish, Patrick had zipped over to a convenience store, picked up a Cosmic Cola—a soft drink that tasted like Coke but had four times the caffeine—and returned.

"Here, drink this."

$$\maltese$$

Lacene hit the ground first, while Luc was still yelling at her about her power.

"How do you *know* you can't reach that far?"

"Well, for starters," she barked, dusting herself off, "I have no idea where Phillip even is. But also, I've been maxed at ten miles. He's surely farther away than that!"

"Maybe I can help," Luc offered. "Maybe my electromagnetic stuff can somehow amplify your signal. You ever thought about that?"

She paused and then replied honestly, "No."

$$\maltese$$

Ooph!

I heard Emmaline return behind me. I was too focused to stop and address her. I just kept pulling with all my might.

I did hear the voices behind me.

"Is he pulling a subway car?" Bentley breathed. *Oh hey, Bentley's here!*

"Looks like it," Emm said, a bit of pride in her voice. "Hey, I need to go look for Greta and Echo. You can hold down the fort here?"

"Um, yeah," Penelope said, not sounding confident.

"Yeah, yeah," Bentley agreed, sounding more like a sports fan than a superhero.

Ooph!

$$\maltese$$

"Just trust me, sis," Luc begged. "It's safe to say he's on Manhattan Island. That's only three miles farther than your supposed cap."

"The cap isn't supposed—it's measured by fine equipment."

"Then let's give it a boost!" he smiled, bending over. "Come on, piggyback ride like when we were kids. Let's go, sis."

"This is so embarrassing." She sighed before jumping up on her brother's back.

"Now, whatever thought you want to send to Phillip, you think that thought hard and send it to me."

Lacene closed her eyes and focused. She took a few deep breaths. She was a good telepath, and she knew how to calm her pulse and prepare for the moment. "I'm ready," she finally said.

"Hit it," Luc said as he engaged his EMP abilities, aiming them at Manhattan.

Both of them screamed, from pain or just screaming out of hope that this would work.

⚡

With more effort than I would care to admit, I finally pulled the subway car all the way back to the terminal.

People poured off in droves, and EMTs ran up with a stretcher to help tend to the pregnant woman.

I slumped down along the wall to catch my breath.

"That can't be the only subway car stuck in the tunnels," I heard Bentley say to Penelope, matter-of-factly.

He was right. Even if every car didn't have a pregnant woman . . . they were all full of humans with destinations and needs and anxieties. "Yeah," I said.

"What?" Bentley leaned down to clarify my comment.

"You're right," I said. "Let's find some other stuck cars and bring them in to the terminal."

Suddenly I heard a voice in my mind. *Phillip, it's Lacene. We're at Coney Island. Can you hear me?*

The Frenchies! I was exuberant. *Yes, yes, I can hear you*, I thought as hard as I could. *Can you hear me?*

There was no reply. *Can you hear me?* I thought again, before being overridden by Lacene's message being repeated.

Phillip, it's Lacene. We're at Coney Island. Can you hear me?

"The twins," I said aloud. "They're talking to my mind, but they can't hear my replies."

Suddenly, a rush of wind. "Hey, morons." It was Patrick. "Freddie and Patrick reporting for duty."

Though I was happy so many of my friends had been found and we were reuniting, I was still facing a tidal wave of new information to process. I was still trying to save some citizens' lives in addition to putting my team back together.

An explosion burst forth from above and cut through everything. A grenade or two had been deployed on the third floor, and figures in red-and-black camouflage-pattern uniforms were descended on ropes.

"Oh no," Bentley whispered.

Penelope finished his frightened thought. "It's the CCF!"

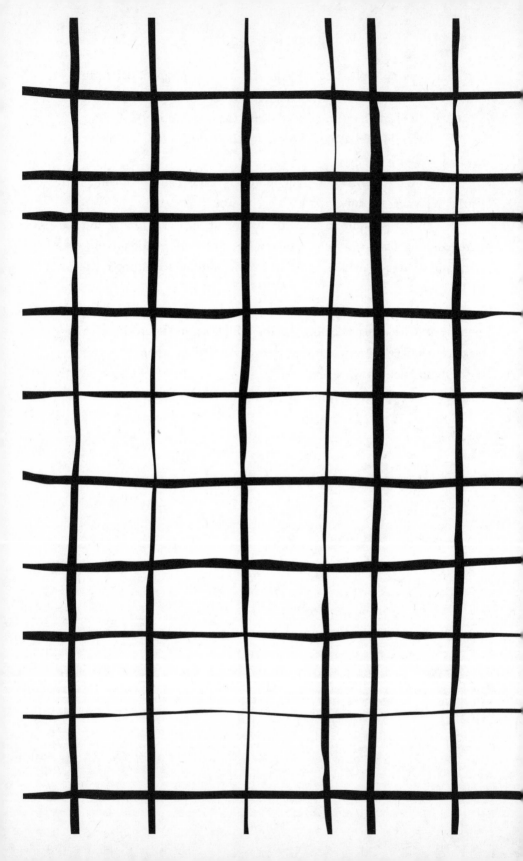

4

THE CCF

The Custodial Containment Force was a real problem for us these days, though it was an entirely illegal use of government finances funding a citizen-led security company.

The CCF's very existence was working its way through the court system, headed for the Supreme Court in a year or two. But for now they were allowed to continue operating due to a lower court ruling.

Essentially it is a group of unregulated "officers" whose stated mission was "to curb and control the activity of empowered custodians in our world." They sought out instances when heroes were saving lives and tried to turn those scenes into conflicts so they could attack us physically and then sue us for attacking them.

They projected an image of custodians as being unnecessarily violent, even while their own violence continued to ramp up.

"How do they keep showing up so fast?" Freddie wondered aloud.

"They have to be tapping into law enforcement feeds," Bentley replied.

The CCF used "nonlethal" means to pursue their agenda. This meant rubber bullets, tear gas, flash bang grenades, and various other options that weren't technically lethal. Technically.

They were a problem for us on multiple levels.

They might shoot us in the head with a rubber bullet—which could kill a person, by the way, despite its nonlethal designation.

But even if they didn't, we still had to subdue them and disarm them without killing *them*. A hero can't kill, at least not unless he has no other choice. A hero is supposed to save lives.

God, I sound like the oath.

Every time they showed up it meant we were doing our job well, and it also meant they would interfere with our ability to continue to do our job well.

Thankfully, the government's pursuit of cost savings had led them to contract out the CCF operations to a robotics company. Each street-level CCF "officer" was an advanced robot being controlled by a human operator back on base.

"Are these the new ones? The robots?" I asked to anyone who might know the answer.

"Let me scan," Bentley responded.

"Scan quickly!" I added urgently.

"They are robots," Bentley finally concluded, sounding impressed. Bentley was an inventor himself, of course, or he used to be. He had invented several robots, though none this sophisticated. He hadn't invented in a while, though, as far as I knew.

"Pat, I need you to run out to Coney Island and bring back the Frenchies," I barked.

"So much running," he said, pretending to hate it.

"Just go, you glory hound," I yelled, and he finally took off.

I heard a whoosh as Bentley raised his hand—as though we were in class. "Um, what's the plan to deal with these CCF agents?"

"Well," I replied, "we have my pushing, Freddie's gigantism, and Penelope's ice and snow. That should hold them off long enough for me to rescue at least one or two more stranded subway cars, right?"

"You also have my brain, which is enhanced, and I think that is a tenuous plan at best," Bentley countered.

"Let's start with a mix of fog, snow, ice, and rain," Penelope advised.

"As usual," Bentley smiled, "the lady is correct *and* has the floor."

⚡

Emmaline started with the Met. It was the most famous arts attraction in New York City, and Emm was nothing if not systematic.

But the Met was also large—humongous, actually. So it took several seconds for her to pop from room to room and shout Greta's and Echo's names. And even if Echo was in the room, she wouldn't be able to audibly respond!

After going around two times, Emm still wasn't sure she'd actually covered all the rooms, but she reasoned it was time to move on to other targets.

No one else was where they said they'd be tonight, why should you two be any different, Emm fumed silently.

It took Patrick all of six seconds to run from the subway station to Coney Island, during which time he had this thought: *I am so awesome.*

That's about a half second per mile, so yes . . . Patrick was wicked fast.

As soon as he arrived, he started doing that shouting thing that had worked so well for finding Freddie. And it worked here just as well. It took him only three "Frenchies!" before he heard their reply.

"I've never used my speed powers with more than one other person," Pat said, suddenly concerned.

"Well, maybe you take us one at a time," Lacene offered. "How long did it take you to get here?"

Patrick was nothing if not brutally honest. "About five seconds."

"Did you say seconds?" Lacene inquired.

"Well, then, maybe we should consider—" Before she finished, she was whisked up into Pat's arms and raced to Manhattan.

I groaned aloud while straining to pull another subway car—this one from the southbound B tunnel—back to the station.

Freddie had gone large—that was his preferred phrasing about his power, "going large"—and was punching CCF idiot-bots left and right, largely catching the stragglers that got through Penelope's weather blockade.

If only Emm were here, I could wipe out those CCF guys quick and just worry about saving stranded train cars.

But Emm wasn't there, so I had to clear my mind of thoughts like this, focusing more and more on the train itself.

"Hey, everyone, Lacene on the scene," Lacene announced with a shout as Patrick dropped her off and went back for her brother.

"Excellent," I nearly shouted. "Can you get in the minds of this first wave of CCF bots—or the dudes nearby controlling them? Maybe fog them up, confuse them?" We knew the CCF robot officers had human controllers and that there was enough data being transferred that they had to be close. "I need you to buy some more time so I can pull in as many train cars as possible."

"Can do," she replied. She immediately jumped into action.

One of my favorite things about my Ables friends was how quickly they would drop real life to rescue one another.

We disagreed on multiple individual issues, but we always agreed on leaping into battle together.

Emmaline continued her logical line of searching for Greta and Echo. The two had intended to visit an art museum, so Emm targeted all other popular NYC art houses and museums.

Turns out there were a lot to choose from.

Emm hit the Guggenheim, the Museum of Modern Art, the Museum of Natural History, *and* the Frick Collection.

She almost gave up. But coming out of the Frick Collection she saw a flyer for a pop-up exhibit in Central Park and decided to check it out.

$\frac{4}{7}$

"What's up?" Pat said, with no context.

"What!" Luc was understandably on edge. His sister had just disappeared.

"Oh," Pat realized, as though his brain was a few seconds behind his body. "It's me, Patrick . . . Phillip's brother. Remember me? I'm here to save you and stuff."

"What?"

Pat's cheery disposition persisted. "I just popped up here a few seconds ago and grabbed your sister and took her to where all the other Ables are. Now I'm here for you."

"What!"

$$\pmb{\mathbf{\mathit{\lightning}}}$$

"They're breaking through, Phillip," Penelope warned me as her ice wall finally gave way to the CCF forces chipping away at it from the outside.

"Freddie," I said, "I've brought two trains into the station. There's at least one more nearby on the third tunnel. Can you try and buy me some time and beat ass on those fools?"

I could hear his smile from two hundred yards away. "I can indeed, sir." He thumped his chest twice and then dove like Pete Rose, headfirst, at the oncoming CCF officers.

$$\pmb{\mathbf{\mathit{\lightning}}}$$

Emmaline approached the temporary stage, alongside a few hundred other spectators.

A man with killer dreadlocks was giving a passionate speech about recycling, and for a moment she thought this was what they were here for.

Once he'd gone backstage, Emm started yelling for Greta and Echo. Sure enough, around the second turn of the path, Greta and Echo were found sitting on a bench together.

"Don't move," Emmaline barked.

"We've been sitting here for two hours. Why would we move?" Greta smiled.

"There's a situation," Emm replied.

"Ohhh," Greta said, rich with sarcasm. "A situation."

Freaking hippies, Emm thought to herself.

"Yippee," Patrick yelled upon his arrival. "I brought back the EMP dude, and I'm ready for action!"

"Yes," I responded immediately, while still grappling with a subway car. "Go help Freddie take out the CCF soldiers, best you can without getting killed—*or* killing any humans!"

"Who do you think you're talking to?" Pat sneered. He darted off and joined the fray. I wasn't truly worried about him, because he was so darn fast I felt like he'd be able to get out of most situations.

His favorite methods of causing mayhem were "knocking out the legs" and "making them think I'm over there when I'm really over here." He also loved turning the angles of evildoers' guns, swords, knives, cannons, and other weapons.

This train in the third tunnel was actually three trains coupled together. It didn't necessarily mean I had to try three times harder, but it did make things more difficult for me. It was all about concentration. And the longer I was able to concentrate, the better. Though time wasn't the only factor. If distractions were at a minimum and I was unfettered, I could work even faster.

Suddenly Emmaline reappeared with Greta and Echo, and we were finally all together.

"What's up?" Greta yelled. "Am I needed?"

"Yes!" I responded instantly. "Go blind all the CCF soldiers attacking us—the people behind the robots; the radio broadcast for all the robots is coming from the third floor of the mall."

"I can do a beam that covers up there and the other floors as well," she offered.

"Do it!" I screamed.

And then suddenly, without warning, I had a panic attack and passed out standing up, only to fall deadweight to the ground.

I awoke to chaos. Fire and noise from every direction. I heard a voice—was it Emmaline?—explaining the situation to me. "You passed out. Freddie dragged the train cars into the station. We're done, but we can't leave because the CCF presence broke through Penelope's weather barrier and set up shop."

I was typically slow to wake up and acclimate to new surroundings. But this time I was sure of my first move. "Emm?"

"Right here," she said, bumping my shoulder with hers to let me know she was right beside me.

I sat up.

Everyone in the room lurched to stop me, concerned about my well-being.

"Just lie down," a doctor or nurse said. "You need to rest."

"I may need to rest," I declared, "but I can't do that right now." I stood. "Emm?" I reached out my hand, and she clasped it. "Shall we try out the latest version of The System?" I asked.

"Let's go," she replied.

5

THE SYSTEM

Ever since Henry's death, I'd been fully blind again.

I hated it.

It made me far less useful on the battlefield and also in the supermarket and basically everywhere I went.

But Bentley had noticed something back during our NASA break-in four years ago; he'd recognized a kind of cooperative relationship between Emm and I.

And so these days we used The System.

The System had four data points. The first was directional. Where was the threat coming from, horizontally speaking?

That data point ranged from 0 to 180, left to right. So the first part of The System's code was the directional degree.

Next came the vertical. We ultimately settled on 10 vertical levels of vision, from the ground to straight up. That was the second data point of The System.

The third factor was the type of telekinesis required. As it so happened, I was able to use my mind to push objects, pull objects, or move them free-form. So the third section of the code was Pull or Push or Grab.

Finally, the fourth element of the code was about power, or total force. It was a scale of 1 to 10 again. So if I wanted to force-push some foot soldiers attacking on my left, I might call out 45-2-push-6.

"45-2-push-6!" Emm's voice was urgent but stoic. I lifted my left arm up and followed her instructions, ultimately zapping four robotic CCF agents charging on our left with guns drawn.

"Do the same thing 20 degrees right!" she barked.

And I obeyed like a computer, sweeping my right arm to the right 20 degrees and firing off another volley of stun-level pushes.

Some more CCF agent-bots started rappelling down from the third story.

Emm barked out new orders. "30-and-6-push-10 and strafe right and left!" The "and" between 30 and 6 was part of the code, to help me know she meant 30 and then 6, as opposed to 36.

I did as she asked. So great was my trust in Emmaline that I could be obliterating a group of adorable puppies right now and I would never know because I just did what she told me.

Granted, Emmaline was an animal lover and unlikely to ever ask me to use my powers against puppies, but still . . . the point about my blind compliance remained.

A small reinforcement squad of CCF officers appeared overhead, sky-diving into the battle zone.

Emmaline wasted no time. "135-8-push-10, 140-8.5-push-10, 137-7.5-push-10!" The commands came hard and fast but I had mastered the shorthand and reacted in near real time, popping off the enemies encroaching on our latest tech.

A sudden new wave of bots rushed in from the tunnels, and Emmaline just went off. She grabbed my shirtsleeve and pointed each arm where she liked, only barking out the type of power and strength.

The left arm went up to chest height. "Push—110 percent, keep it flowing." My right arm was jerked upward by Emm's control. "Same," she shouted. "Now!" she yelled. Her impatience was a quality I hated and adored.

I let loose with both hands, full blasting my push abilities. Emmaline, controlling both arms via her clutching hands, dragged them left and then right, back and forth.

We obliterated those things. CCF bots went flying to and fro, breaking against the subway walls by the sheer force of my push power. Some hit the ceiling. Others crashed into other bots. Some tumbled back down dark subway tunnels.

To the casual observer, it probably looked like an apocalypse. Metal parts of former CCF bots echoed down the long subway tunnels as they bounced and careened toward obscurity.

"It might be time to leave," Bentley shouted.

"He's right," Emm stated before barking out more orders. "100-9-push—oh forget it." Emmaline grabbed my right arm with both her hands, pointed it at the bad guys, and yelled, "*Full power push!*"

My subconscious kicked in and did what it was told, as Emm sprayed my pushing power around by swinging my arms left and right in tiny intervals. Finally she let go of my sleeves, and I instinctively cut off my powers.

I took a few deep breaths, then turned. Emm stood upright and panted a bit.

Emm and I finally grabbed hands in solidarity and turned around, toward the other Ables, who were speechless. Apparently our combined battle technique had surprised or offended everyone, because we were met with total silence for about five or six seconds.

"Wow," Greta finally exhaled. "That was . . . frightening."

"Are you sure you got 'em all?" Patrick asked, sarcastically.

"I'm so tired of dealing with those things," I growled. "I'm ready to deal with the humans controlling them."

Luc seemed to agree. "Remind me never to piss you guys off."

"We need to get out of here," Bentley urged as another round of CCF forces descended from street level down the staircase into the mall. He was right. The benefit to the CCF of using robot officers was that they could be a largely never-ending source of law enforcement. One went down and another came up. The robots didn't have to be super smart, since their movements were controlled by a human counterpart, likely on a nearby mobile command vehicle, safe on a military base six miles away.

"He's right. Everyone in!"

⚡

Seconds later we were all standing in Charles Field back in our home of Freepoint. Yes, college classes began the next morning in Goodspeed, but that was the luxury of having a friend who can teleport—you can save on room and board by living at home and zapping to campus every morning.

Bentley and I walked along the sidewalk as Patrick raced ahead and Emmaline teleported some of the others home.

"You two are something fierce together," he said. "There's so much raw power between you—it's something to see."

"You sound concerned." Sherpa led me down into the street by the curb for a few steps, then back up onto the sidewalk. It was common for her to help me avoid potential tripping sources, even if that sometimes required a step up or down.

"Not concerned. Impressed. Maybe a little jealous. Maybe a little scared."

"They're just robots, Bent," I said.

"Yeah," he sighed. "But they might not always be. If those had been human combatants . . . you'd have killed most of them."

"If those had been human combatants we would have dialed back the severity of the attack," I countered.

"Fair enough," I could hear him nodding.

Just then Emm showed up.

Ooph!

"Hey, guys," she said.

"Get everyone home?" I asked.

"Yep. Got a little waylaid at the Frenchies' house. Is it just me that their foster mother tries to feed every time I'm over there?"

"No," Bentley and I said in unison.

"The woman has a feeding obsession," I added.

"I think it's a French thing," Bentley stated.

"That's racist," I joked.

Bentley ignored me. "Listen, you guys have sure taken the system we developed and fine-tuned it like a well-oiled machine," he said, sounding impressed.

"Thanks," Emm smiled.

"And as much as I may live to regret this later, I think I figured out a way to make it even more streamlined."

"Yeah?" I asked, betraying my curiosity.

"If I'm right, I think I can cut maybe two of your four data points in the language you're speaking. But I don't want to say much more until I dive a little deeper into my sketches and build a prototype."

"A prototype!" I was beyond impressed. "A physical invention? You're building us a machine?"

"I'm building a couple machines, but no . . . this would be . . . a wearable enhancement."

I was momentarily distracted by what he'd said. "You . . . you're back to inventing?" After the events in DC, Bentley had been fighting his own demons. I wrestled with Henry's death, but Bentley had to also make sense of the fact that his father had been one of the custodians that had flipped and was involved in the evil plot we ultimately foiled.

And it rocked him.

Bentley's lifestyle, and all his family's riches, came from his father. Every invention he had ever built had been paid for by his father. Discovering that those monies had been ill-gotten had caused Bentley to give up inventing.

I was glad my friend was back to one of his favorite activities.

"The point," Bentley said, in an attempt to redirect the conversation, "is that I have an idea for you two that might help you communicate even more fluidly on the battlefield."

"Well I, for one, can't wait to see it," Emm said cheerily.

"Me too," I agreed.

"Alright, this is my turn," Bentley called. "I'll see you tomorrow." He turned to walk the rest of the way to his neighborhood.

The three of us had done this routine enough to know that if Emmaline asked if Bentley wanted to teleport home, he would say no. So she didn't ask anymore. We figured Bentley enjoyed the alone time to think and that he enjoyed being able to get around on his own power, for as long as he was able to do so. Eventually, he'd told us, he'd lose enough mobility in his legs and arms to need a wheelchair, but he seemed determined to hold that day off by sheer force of will.

Emmaline and I continued a few moments in silence.

We tended to walk to my house in instances like this—returning from a trip or a battle—because she could zap home instantly once I'd gone inside. She said she liked walking me home.

"Do you want to talk any more about the dreams?" she asked softly.

"Not really," I admitted.

"I just think it's important you acknowledge them and address them." She grabbed my hand. "Have you told your therapist about them yet?"

"No," I admitted again.

"I think you should," she nudged, lovingly.

"I know," I agreed.

"You've done therapy for years. What are you afraid of?"

"I'm afraid she's going to agree with me and say Henry's death was my fault."

Emm started to object, as she had so many times before when I'd put the blame for Henry's death on me. But then she stopped herself, squeezed my hand, and simply said, "I'm really sorry you had to go through that."

We'd reached my house, and she hugged me—harder and longer than usual.

"I'll pick you and Patty up here tomorrow at eight, okay?"

"Okay." I smiled.

Ooph!

She disappeared.

I have the coolest girlfriend ever, I thought.

I sat on the stoop for a moment, Sherpa finally knowing I felt safe enough she could ask for rubs like a normal dog. I scrubbed her neck and back while thinking about Emm's words.

How do I move beyond something so terrible? How do I forgive myself for such an awful mistake?

Sherpa didn't seem to think I needed forgiveness, as she started licking my hand, then my cheek. In reality she probably knew we were home and was hungry as hell.

I stood up, entered my key, and walked in the front door.

"Hello, Phillip," my dad chuckled nervously. "Welcome home."

He walked over and hugged me.

Something was off. I could smell a candle and a slightly burnt casserole of some kind. And wine. And perfume.

Then it all clicked. Dad was on a date. Dad brought a date home to this house and cooked her dinner. A date!

This was too much information for me to process all at once.

Sure, Mom had been gone a while now, and Dad was certainly entitled to date. But it was still unexpected. And maybe Dad could have prepped me for this a little better.

Also, I was exhausted from a camping trip that had turned into a draining custodial rescue. My girlfriend was mad at me, my best friend was keeping inventions and other secrets from me . . .

Maybe I just wasn't in the right state of mind to walk in on a Daddy date.

"Hello, Phillip," said the woman, who sounded very friendly. "It's so nice to finally meet you."

And my second panic attack in twenty-four hours hit me like a ton of bricks. I slumped to the floor, front door still wide open, leaving my father and his date to deal with the fallout.

That night I had another Henry dream.

This time he was in a clergy's gown.

"You know what you did," he preached from behind a pulpit made of white marble. "God knows what you did."

Suddenly Echo appeared as an altar girl, and she ran up to me and whisper-yelled in my ear, "It's all a game, Phillip."

Then she skipped down the aisle giggling and darted out the door.

6

THE FIRST SPEECH

"C'est le meilleur sandwich que j'ai jamais goûté!" Luc cried between bites.

I didn't know for certain what he had said, but I was sure he was praising the quality of the food. Goodspeed University didn't mess around on the food. Everything was excellent, which was clearly reflected in the outrageous tuition bills all students received upon graduation.

Goodspeed was twice the size of Freepoint, and the most populated of all custodian cities around the globe. Of course, a large portion of its residents consisted of students at the university.

The food court offered a hot and cold sandwich shop, a Mexican place, a burgers-and-fries American option, an Italian counter, and a sushi bar.

"So what do we know about the power outage in New York?" I asked, mostly to Bentley, though other members had also done some research.

"Statewide," Bentley replied. "The whole state lost power at the exact same time."

"How is that even possible?" Lacene asked. "My brother can kill power to maybe a one- or two-mile radius. There's no EMP that can kill a whole state."

"What happens in an outage that big?" I asked. "Where does all that power go?"

"It has to go somewhere, right? It can't just disappear," Freddie offered.

"Yes, it has to go somewhere," Bentley confirmed. "With most natural power outages, it's a blast of lightning hitting a transformer and giving off a massive spark. But there wasn't a storm here. No lightning."

"So where did New York's power go?" I half-demanded.

"I don't know," Bentley admitted. "It's gone, and it shouldn't be gone. Energy can't just disappear. It went somewhere, but I haven't figured it out yet."

"So we don't know if this was an accident or intentional?" I asked.

Bentley's voice suggested he'd turned to look at me. "Intentional?"

"It seems just fishy enough not to be random."

"Occam's razor," he countered.

Occam's razor, boiled down, is that the simplest solution is usually the correct one.

"Maybe it was a meteorite!" Patrick blurted out.

"Don't be ridiculous," Luc replied. "It was obviously aliens."

Most everyone laughed or chuckled.

"I think we should move on and use this lunch hour as it was intended," Freddie declared, "to help me understand this physics homework." He slapped his textbook on the table, knowing full well Bentley would take the bait and swoop in to explain things.

I sauntered off to the food line because I was actually hungry during lunch hour, which was rare. Usually lunchtime made me nauseous. Lunch hadn't been a regular meal for me for years. My therapist thinks I formed some unhealthy habits about meals during a time of trauma healing. She was probably right; she was always right.

It was weird being in college. I was smart enough to pass all my classes, and I wondered what job that knowledge was supposed to prepare me for when I was a superhero.

Nevertheless, I majored in speech communications. There were a lot of subareas in that field that held interest for me: theater, music, radio, and TV. Also the advisor last year told me a lot of freshmen pick speech communications as their major when they aren't sure what else they want to pick.

I headed for the cold sandwich line. A ham and cheese would do nicely. I couldn't put anything too risky in my stomach because I had Dr.

Gates for Speech 2 this afternoon. Dr. Gates loved impromptu speeches and was notorious for popping them on students on the first day of a new semester.

Dr. Gates was also my advisor, now that I had picked a major in her field, and I'd had two classes with her last year. She was one of the best teachers I'd ever had. Smart, passionate about the topics, goofy but still wise. It's corny, but she was the kind of professor that made you excited to learn more. But she was also tough as nails.

"Nice. Is it bring your dog to school day?" I didn't recognize the voice, but I did pick up on the snarky tone. It changed immediately, probably because he got close enough to read. "Oh, sorry man. I didn't realize."

"No worries," I said.

Sherpa had a vest, and on both sides it said "I am a service dog. I'm working now, so please don't pet me." Now, Sherpa didn't need the vest. A lot of service dogs use the vest as their signal to differentiate between work time and play time, so when the vest comes off, it's time to run around and be a dog. Sherpa just knew instinctively. She really was borderline supernatural in some ways.

I put the vest on her in public mostly so people would leave me alone. Obviously it hadn't worked this time.

"Aren't you in Dr. G's Speech 2 class in a couple hours?" he asked. "Sorry, I wasn't spying," he explained. "I was just in line behind you at the registrar's office.

"Yeah," I said, stepping forward one step as Sherpa indicated the line had moved. "I am. I'm Phillip." I stuck out my hand.

"I'm Nate. Nate Weller. You—your last name is Sallinger, right?"

"Yep, that's me." I'd gotten used to people viewing me with a hint of celebrity. I'd been in enough high-profile encounters I was just more well-known than other kids my age.

"You're kind of a big deal, aren't you?" He wasn't making fun, at least I didn't think he was.

"Not if you ask my brother," I replied. I'd worked up a handful of cheeky responses to questions like these over the years.

"Why does a guy like you wanna major in speech comm?"

I shrugged as Sherpa led me forward another few steps. "Gotta major in something, I guess. Right? I don't have any real passionate reason for picking it. Do you?"

"Oh yeah," he said, his voice climbing and diving ever so slightly, letting me know he was nodding. "I want to be a journalist, man. I want to cover the news—specifically custodial news."

"That's awesome."

"Listen," he said, "I heard a rumor about an impromptu speech on this first day of class. What do you know?"

"Haven't you had Dr. G before?"

"No, I just transferred in. Freshman year I went to State."

"State?"

"Oh, I'm not a custodian. I don't have any powers or anything," he explained. He talked so fast it was jarring.

"Oh," I said, somewhat surprised.

Human-support personnel from any custodial city or base were allowed to send their kids to any of the three custodial universities, but otherwise nonempowered kids weren't typically admitted.

Nate must have guessed what I was thinking or simply had similar conversations like this before, because he continued explaining to fill in the gaps.

"I had to go to State first year because I couldn't get a hearing on Goodspeed admittance until that January, and I didn't want to fall behind." Nate was either a fast talker or he'd had too much caffeine at lunch. "Anyway, I had the hearing and they gave me a waiver to go to school here—I think mostly because my specific journalism passion is about custodians and how the world reacts to them. We're in such an exciting and pivotal time in human civilization, I think, and I'm super excited to be one of the people covering it all from a news standpoint."

I stepped forward again, and it was suddenly my turn to order. "Well, it's been nice chatting. I'll see you in class," I offered.

"Okay, great. I'll see you there." And with that, Nate was gone, probably speed-walking.

"What can I get you?" the cashier asked, sounding already bored of her job on just the first day.

"Ham and cheese, please."

⚡

Goodspeed University had a lovely campus. Beautiful. And I do think blind people can tell when a place is beautiful.

I could smell the generous flower beds and the various trees along the walkways. I could hear the wide variety of wild bird calls—even an occasional owl from just inside the nearby woods.

I could feel the low humidity. I could feel the cobblestones beneath my feet.

Believe me, I may have understood the campus's beauty more than most sighted students. Maybe not. But I liked to think that a silver lining to the blindness was that I was better able to appreciate the information relayed by the other four senses.

I was sitting on a wooden bench just outside a jogging path that ran along the Goodspeed River—which, as Bentley was fond of reminding anyone who would listen, was not actually a river. It was a man-made tributary designed to run through the center of the campus and make everyone feel more peaceful. Bentley's favorite fact about it was that the Goodspeed River had been tested earlier in the decade and found to be more polluted than any other North American waterway.

How polluted? The river contained no species of fish or other water creatures. It was literally a chemistry experiment floating by students who were too stressed to care if a river was pretty or not. A few dozen seniors still always jumped into it after graduation every year.

"What do you think?" I asked. "Should I do the 'Phillip is totally a normal person' introduction speech or the 'Phillip has seen some shit so please like him' version?"

Sherpa lifted her head off my lap, wondering if I was saying anything about her, which I was not, so she returned to her slumber.

Most first-day-of-class impromptu speeches were introductory—tell us about yourself, make it informative and interesting and entertaining. Even in high school I'd shown a little interest in this course of study and had taken Speech and Debate. I had two versions of my introduction ready to go and was hoping I could really impress Dr. Gates this year.

I heard a faint familiar noise, knowing immediately what it meant. I waited a few more seconds for her to get close enough to hear and then I asked Sherpa another question.

"Sherps . . . do you think Emmaline has any idea how loud her teleporting is?"

"Alright," Emm said in defeat. "You heard me again?"

"I did. I don't even think it's my hearing. I think teleporting is just louder than you realize, because you're the teleporter. Being on the inside, you can't know what it sounds like on the outside."

We'd been playing a version of this game for a few years now. She wanted desperately to sneak up on me and surprise me, but she didn't want to teleport in too far away from my location, because then it would just be like sneaking up on me by walking, which anyone could do—or try.

"I had a few seconds, thought I'd see if you were here. You worried about your speech?" I don't know what Emmaline saw when she looked at me, but I assumed it was a kind of teleprompter of my thoughts, detailing my state of mind at the moment, because she was *always* right.

"I don't even know that there will be a speech, but it's got me all in knots." I always got nervous before a speech in class, but then a minute or so into the thing I always felt calm and composed. I couldn't explain it.

She sat down next to me. "Well, I would tell you to try picturing everyone in the audience in their underwear, but . . ." She was making a rare joke, one only she or Patrick could get away with—or James back in the day—pointing out my limitations as a blind person.

"Ha ha ha ha ha, you jerk," I laughed.

"There you go," she replied. "Now carry that smile into class and knock 'em dead." She kissed my cheek, and then I heard—

Ooph!

As it turned out, we did have to give impromptu speeches in Dr. G's Speech

2 class on the first day. However, they were not the standard introductory speeches. Instead, we all pulled from a hat and had to give a speech for or against whatever topic was on our paper.

My new acquaintance, Nate, ended up going before me. He pulled climate change as a topic. And much to my chagrin, "speech class Nate" spoke every bit as slowly as "regular Nate" did fast. It was pretty excruciating.

After every speech, Dr. G was giving impromptu grades—"Not fair to ask you to do this on the spot if I'm not willing to judge you on the spot," she'd said.

After Nate's molasses marathon about whales and glaciers, Dr. G said, "We need to find a way to speed up your speaking, but I thought a good bit of your content was solid."

Nate replied as he walked back to his seat, now back to speaking super quickly. "Oh, thanks, thanks a lot, I really appreciate the constructive criticism and I'll be sure to work it into my next speech, you'll see."

Dr. Gates simply mumbled a confused. "Hmm."

Soon enough, no matter what I willed, it was my turn. Most times, the benefit of going near the end is that the teacher is probably tired and you have a good chance of just fading from their memory altogether. In this case, the downside to going last was that most of the decent topics had already been pulled out of the hat.

I reached in, and there seemed to be two papers left. I assumed one was awesome and one sucked, and that I would definitely end up grabbing the sucky one.

I pinched one and pulled it out of the hat. Since I was the only blind student in class, there was no protocol here yet. I just turned the paper around for those in the front row to see and hoped one of them would tell me what it said.

And I got lucky.

"Homelessness," a girl before me stated.

I let out an obnoxious sigh before I finally began. I started with the intro we'd been instructed to use: "Hi, I'm Phillip Sallinger, and my topic is homelessness." From there I was expected to begin my ninety-second speech.

"Homelessness," I stated.

So far so good, moron.

"Homelessness should be easy to eradicate." I was just saying what came to mind, while mostly still thinking about things like New York or Henry or my dad dating again. "And yet it's not."

Why is my mind so scattered right now?

I heard a throat clear, a cough, and a few doodles being drawn.

"Instead, in cities like Boston and San Francisco, homelessness is at an all-time high." I didn't have any statistical or factual knowledge here, I was just winging it, on total autopilot.

A janitor wheeled a squeaky mop bucket past the door. A gum wrapper crackled from the direction of the girl who'd read my paper out for me.

"Um," I said before I could stop myself. *Oh crap, "um" is one of the seven deadly sins of giving public speeches!* I tried to cover it up by racing forward. "There's more than enough money to fix the homeless problem . . . I think."

I think? I think! I hated myself in the moment. This was a very bad speech, even though it was still so painfully young.

More coughing. Maybe the coughing student was trying to serve as a road sign to me, to change directions. Like, "Phillip, no! Turn around now!"

Maybe someone just had a cold.

How long has it been since I spoke? I wondered. *Oh god, it's been too long, hasn't it?*

"Um."

Dagnabbit!

"Homeless people just want . . ." I went through a host of nouns and somehow settled on "love."

Stop talking right now, I screamed internally.

"In summation," my mouth continued without permission, "homelessness is bad, and we should . . ." I felt a wave of dizziness. "We should . . ." I reached out for the desk to steady myself. "Fix . . ." I keeled over and hit the floor.

My third panic attack in three days. How embarrassing. At least it's tough to fail a speech when you have a medical emergency in the middle of it.

7

THE DOCTORS

I awoke in the Freepoint Hospital—the same room I'd stayed in twice before. Granted, I was sort of a usual customer at this hospital, due to my tendency to disregard my own safety. Additionally, it was a pretty small hospital in a pretty small town, so the odds of landing in the same room were better than one might think.

Apparently my recent rash of pass-out panic attacks had worried my friends and Dr. Gates, and an ambulance had been called and I'd been transferred to Freepoint.

I woke up quietly enough that no one noticed. Emmaline was on the couch to my right, whispering with Penelope. In the corner stood Patrick, Freddie, and Bentley, murmuring about something.

The next corner over, I could hear Dad and his new girlfriend as well as Luc and Lacene conversing.

"Listen," I said, just to get their attention. "My speech wasn't as bad as you've probably heard," I continued with a smile.

Everyone laughed nervously and approached the bed to check on me. It was actually chaos for a bit, until a nurse came in and barked for everyone to leave.

A few seconds later, it was only Dad and me remaining.

What are you doing? I asked myself. *How long can you act like nothing's wrong?*

The door opened, and a pair of doctors entered.

"Hello, Phillip, I'm Dr. Marvin, and this is Dr. Pulaski. We're here to talk to you about your health."

"Great," I managed. "Hit me."

"Your panic attacks have been increasing lately," Dr. Marvin's voice declared.

A new voice then responded, female; I assumed this was Pulaski. "Panic attacks are one thing, but we are equally concerned about the damage being done to your body and mind every time you pass out."

"You're not going to ask me to name the presidents or walk in a straight line, are you?" My sarcasm should have been evident, though in my tired state I worried I hadn't given it enough emphasis.

"Phillip," Dad scolded, using a single word to ask me to be more cooperative with the medical professionals.

"We just want to help you pass out less." It was Dr. Marvin's voice.

"Maybe a change in anxiety medication," Dr. Pulaski suggested.

I sighed long and deep.

People who had no mental health issues had no idea how hard it was for us to find the right medication or to find a medication that would work for more than a few months before becoming ineffective.

I'd been on my current anxiety meds for two years, and the thought of changing made me cringe. And yet . . . things were getting worse with the blackouts and attacks. Maybe it was time.

"I've been on this one for two years," I explained.

Dad chimed in. "What if we increased the dosage?"

"We can't." It was Pulaski.

Marvin completed the thought. "He's already at the highest dose we're allowed to prescribe."

Now it was Dad's turn to sigh.

"Is there anything else we can do to work with the medication to maybe improve things?" I asked.

"Well, we can look at your diet," Pulaski offered. She was firm, with a hint of warmth. "What kinds of foods you eat and how they interact and break down."

"Exercise," Dr. Marvin added. He was a bit warmer, and I got the sense he was the "good cop" to Pulaski's "bad cop." "How often do you exercise?"

"You mean doing custodian stuff? I just saved a bunch of people in New York during that blackout," I responded, feeling confident I'd aced this particular test.

"No," Pulaski shot me down. "I'm talking about daily sustained exercise like swimming or running. It's great for your body but even better for your mind. Do you play any sports?"

"Yes," I deadpanned. "I'm the football team's starting quarterback and the pitching ace for the baseball team."

"Don't be a smartass," Dad snapped.

"I don't play any sports," I revised. "I'm blind."

"My nephew's blind," Dr. Marvin chimed in, "and he's a champion chess player." There was so much cheer in his voice, it seemed out of place in a hospital.

"Chess isn't a sport," I countered with a bit too much indignation.

"What about a stationary bike or a treadmill?" Pulaski offered, trying to get us back on track. "You can do those things, right?"

"Yeah," I admitted.

"The university even has a state-of-the-art fitness center," Dad offered unhelpfully.

"Great," Marvin added, again seeming genuinely happy.

"There are other things I'd like you to try," Pulaski said flatly, losing her sliver of warmth rapidly. "Meditation, sunshine, breathing exercises, journaling, and therapy."

"Oh," I started, excited to get brownie points. "I'm already doing the therapy. I've been seeing my shrink for about five years now."

The two doctors whispered a bit while Dad came over to do the dad thing. "We'll be out of here soon, son," he said, rubbing my forehead like I was still twelve and not nineteen. Most annoyingly, he made enough noise that I was unable to hear what the doctors were saying.

"We're not mental health professionals," Marvin began, "so we can only offer suggestions. But . . . if you've been in therapy with the same practitioner for that many years and your panic attacks are getting worse and more frequent . . ." he trailed off, perhaps feeling guilty about blasting another professional's work.

But Pulaski was more than up to the task, so she finished the thought. "Maybe you should switch therapists. Maybe your current therapist has done all they can do for you and is only a hindrance at this point."

I glassed over at that, and the rest was Dad talking to the doctors about a follow-up exam in a month and temporary prescriptions to help me sleep.

I just fell into a mental hole.

It made sense for the medical docs to wonder if maybe my therapist had lost her effectiveness. If everything's continuing as normal but the panic attacks and pass-outs are getting worse . . . I mean, any logical person would at least ask the question.

But only I knew the answer was no. My therapist had, in fact, been pushing me to exercise and eat better. My therapist had suggested I look into chain saw art—an idea that terrified me, though she said over and over that the focus required to operate such a dangerous and deadly instrument was a form of meditation.

The truth was that I had stopped listening to my therapist's advice six months ago and had begun to lie to her, telling her I was doing the treadmill and meditating, eating more energy-providing foods. I neglected to tell her about the panic attacks.

And look, she didn't do anything wrong by believing me. Therapy—successful therapy—requires an honest patient. And most therapists assume clients are telling the truth.

The point was, I finally knew why I was having increased attacks: I'd been lazy and had ignored professional advice.

This was all my own fault—and well within my power to reverse and fix. But even walking out to the parking lot with Dad, Dad's date, Patrick, and Emmaline, I wasn't sure I would change anything, at least not in the short term. The depth of my stubbornness was yet to be revealed.

⚡

We dropped Emmaline off first.

I walked her to the door—which for the two of us was kind of a role reversal.

"I'm worried about you," she said softly.

"I know you are. I'm sorry," I replied. "I'm going to make some changes soon, and it'll get better. I promise."

"Well you'd better," she declared, poking me in the chest. "I never feel like myself more than when I'm around you, and if you take that away from me . . . I'll never forgive you."

The porch light came on. Emmaline's father had a terrible sense of humor and an even worse sense of timing. I mean, Emm and I had been friendly for four years and had gone from hanging out to . . . hanging out and sometimes holding hands . . . in *four years*.

We were moving at a glacial pace, as young romances went, and yet her father felt compelled to keep doing the whole protective parent thing. I knew he actually liked me a great deal and he was just having a little fun. It was still annoying.

"Hello, sir," I said loudly, waving at him behind the window. "Good night," I said to Emmaline.

"I'll see you tomorrow," she replied before going inside.

I tapped my way back to the car using my cane, even though I had nearly memorized Emmaline's front sidewalk. There were two potential trip points, both due to cracking of the concrete. I navigated them both smoothly and got back into the car.

Next we dropped off my father's date, a few blocks away at the River Glenn apartments. I was familiar with the area because Freddie lived here.

"We'll be right back," Dad said before shutting his car door and walking off.

I really wasn't mad that Dad was dating. Everything about it was natural and made sense. I was just mad still because my mom was gone. And Dad dating another woman was just a reminder of Mom being gone.

I obviously couldn't see if they walked up to her door holding hands or if they kissed. It was one of the few times I was glad to be blind. Patrick would be seeing it right now and getting made fun of by me later had he not scored an early ride home with Freddie.

I'd had an eventful day, but only here and now, alone in the car, did I realize Sherpa wasn't with me. It was an uneasy feeling, as I'd grown accustomed to her presence.

Just then Dad opened the driver's door and climbed back into the car. I'd expected his good-night to his date to take longer, so I was caught off guard momentarily, before remembering my most pressing issue. "Dad, where's Sherpa?"

"Patrick took her home," he replied nonchalantly as he pulled out of the parking lot. "The doctors were having a hard time getting their tests done. That dog really loves you, kid," he said, chuckling, having no idea how right he was.

"Okay, good. As long as she's alright, I guess. But I'm definitely going to kill Pat if he gave her potato chips again."

There was a long silence as we drove a block and a half. Finally Dad spoke again.

"Do you think it's okay for me to be dating again, son?" He turned left down Watson Street. "Because if you had a problem with it, I think I would understand that, and I'd want to try and talk it out."

I groaned for a solid five or ten seconds, not really wanting to have this conversation. "Ehhhhhhh, I think you should follow your heart, Dad."

"You do?"

"I miss Mom. So realizing you're dating this woman briefly made me think of Mom, which made me sad that she's gone. But that's not your fault. I want you to be happy, Dad. I don't want you to be alone."

"Wow," he replied. "I didn't expect that kind of support. But I'm thankful for it. You know I love you kids. I loved your mom. I don't want anyone to be hurt."

"I think you've got more work ahead of you with Patrick than you did with me," I said honestly.

We both were silent for a couple blocks.

"So who is she?" I finally asked, realizing I didn't know anything about this woman my father was suddenly spending time with.

I could hear Dad smile even before he spoke. "Her name is Wendy. Wendy Sisco. She's human support, and she works at the administrative office downtown."

"How did you meet?"

"We met at the Freepoint Grocery, actually. It's pretty cliché, but we met in the produce section of the supermarket." He sounded so authentically into this woman as he told the story, I found it hard to stay wary.

Finally I heard him reach up and punch the garage door opener just before pulling into our driveway.

"I'm sorry if I was standoffish to her or about her," I offered as an olive branch. "I just still miss Mom, and I guess I get triggered easily."

"I get it," he said before shutting off the car and closing the garage door. "You can always be honest with me. Always."

"I know, Dad," I acknowledged. "You too."

That night my dreams turned competitive.

I was playing chess against Bentley, while Emmaline played opposite Henry. We were the last four in a chess tournament, and the paparazzi stood by outside waiting to photograph the winners but also the losers.

Playing in Washington Square Park in NYC, we'd attracted a crowd.

Bentley sneered at me. "I'm smarter than you by a factor of one hundred."

Henry trash-talked Emmaline the same. "I can read your mind, girl. How can you hope to surprise me?"

I worked to move all my pieces forward; if my opponent was saying he was smarter, I would meet that intelligence with brute force.

Emmaline, however, had no such gumption. She merely toppled her king right away, defaulting and deferring. No challenge. Henry won the matchup.

The scene shifted to an Oscars-style awards show, and Henry was giving an acceptance speech. "I dedicate this award to the asshole who killed me, my former best friend, Phillip. He believed in me until his own neck was on the line, and then he sold me out."

Henry then held up the statue, turned completely into light, and leaped off stage into the air and up into space.

I woke up hyperventilating. Upon realizing it had been a dream, I collapsed back onto my bed and continued panting and wheezing.

8

THERAPY

"Who do you believe blames you for Henry's death?"

"Anyone with a brain," I replied with a bit of my usual salt.

"Has anyone told you they blame you for Henry's death?" My therapist was patient, and every statement was delivered with the same meter and rhythm.

I thought about it for a moment. "No."

"So the only person you know for sure who blames you for his death is . . . you."

The most frustrating therapy days were like this, where she was right a bunch and I had to agree and then change. Stupid therapy.

Big sigh, then, "Yes."

"So then why do *you* believe his death was your fault?"

"Bad team management. It's my job to keep everyone safe out there. I performed poorly as a leader and led us into a trap."

"Interesting." My therapist loved responding with the word *interesting*. "So without the benefit of any other new information, what do you think you should have done differently? What move could you have made to avoid the same fate?"

I chewed on that one long and hard. Sometimes a silent therapy patient is just being stubborn or uncooperative. Other times it's the exact opposite and they're actually processing, pondering, and maybe even growing.

She filled in the blanks for me. "There's no reason you would ever have known or realized Henry was her true target. And without knowing that . . . there's no move you could have made that would have changed the outcome." She took a deep breath. "You know that, right?"

"But I'm the captain. No matter what, if something bad happens during my team's performance, it's my fault. Always. By definition." I could tell I was faking most of this, but I wasn't sure if she could. "If not for me, Henry is still alive."

"Ah," she sighed. "But that's not really true, is it? Did you not tell me yourself that Henry died by his own doing?"

"Yes, I did." It was a bit more complicated than that, in that Henry had used his mind power to force my brain power to force my hand to drop the rock that crushed him, but she had the gist of it.

"So how is it your fault if it was his doing?" She let that hang in the air about five seconds before shifting gears on me. "Let's talk about the panic attacks." She was also excellent at changing the subject abruptly as a way of keeping the conversation honest, keeping me on my toes. "When was the last one, now, April?"

I sat silent for probably twenty seconds. I knew what I had to do and it sounded so simple: just be honest. But I also knew that she would make me work harder in coming weeks, and I really didn't want to work hard at anything right now.

"What don't you want to tell me?" she finally asked.

"I've had three episodes in the last four days, six in the last two weeks total."

I heard her gasp. She tried to keep it quiet, and she actually did a good job, but I have incredible hearing so I heard it anyway. After a beat, she responded as though she'd expected that answer. "I'm glad you told me that. That's probably been weighing on you."

It had been. I nodded.

"Why do you think you withheld that information from me, Phillip?"

"Because I'm afraid I'm never going to get better. This anxiety, the panic, the PTSD . . . it feels like it's always going to be getting worse, bit by bit."

My therapist always had data to back up her arguments. "Clinical studies have proven time and again that people can improve their anxiety and depression situations through a variety of methods like therapy, medication, exercise."

"Oh yeah," I offered, "I haven't actually been doing the treadmill like I told you." Might as well get it all out there on the table.

There was a huge pause, this time initiated by her.

Is she waiting for me to speak? Is she not sure what to say?

Turned out she just wanted to make sure she struck the right tone for her next statements.

"I can't do my job if you don't tell me the truth."

"I know that—"

"Hush," she cut me off. "I'm talking."

I raised my arms in surrender and leaned back into the couch.

"If you lie to me, you are wasting my time and your own time. And paying for it. Now I told you in our first session I would never give up on you no matter what you did as long as you never gave up on this process. So . . . have you given up on this process?"

"No." I was finally telling her the truth again.

"Good." She sounded relieved. "Now, what else haven't you told me?"

I thought about it a moment. "I think my girlfriend is running out of patience about it."

"Interesting." She wrote something down.

"What's that? What are you writing down?" I asked.

"I'm taking notes, like always."

"But what specifically are you writing? Is it . . . do you know how I can keep her from . . ."

"I wrote down, 'first time he's ever referred to Emmaline as his girlfriend,'" she revealed.

I let out a half laugh, half sigh.

"Phillip," she said firmly, "have you ever heard of EMDR?"

I ran the letters over in my brain a bit but couldn't find an acronym that made sense. So I answered honestly, "No."

"You might consider it," she added. "It's a way of using lights and movement to help the mind destigmatize traumatic memories."

"Sounds expensive," I tossed out lazily.

"It's not," she replied. "I'm concerned that your new rash of panic attacks is driven by PTSD. Basically you went through traumatic events and you still haven't processed them."

"Like what kind of events?"

"Like DC. Henry's death. James's death. The Grand Canyon mess last year. On and on and on, Phillip. You've had enough traumatic events for ten lifetimes."

⚡

It was Saturday, which meant that Dad was off at the weekly meeting of the Custodial Relations Board. It had been established after the confrontation in Washington and was filled with half humans and half custodians.

Any business regarding custodians and their role in society came through this board, and I was generally very proud my father sat in one of those chairs.

But this meant I had no ride home. So Sherpa and I walked. She certainly knew the way home, and I was happy to get a bit of exercise for once, as my therapist had just been harping on me about that.

Emmaline usually could have popped in to pick me up, but she and her family had gone to visit her grandparents a couple states over. She texted me to let me know they all made it there safely, which was just a nerdy joke since she'd teleported her entire immediate family there instantaneously. I kept telling her that if we could round up enough teleporters, we could start up a transportation service that would single-handedly make a sizable dent in carbon emissions.

It was just as well. I needed some alone time. Therapy can be physically and emotionally draining, and often some of the best growth work is done after the session as the patient continues rolling things around that were mentioned.

It wasn't quite yet fall, but the heat of summer had dimmed, and there was a pleasant breeze blowing through town. The sounds of Freepoint were typical for a Saturday. No school buses, less traffic overall since businesses take the weekend off as well. It was just after noon, so the bank was appropriately quiet. The grocery store sounded packed, and Jack's Pizza was full of young athletes in between soccer matches and T-ball games.

A few dogs barked at us as we moved through the neighborhood. Sherpa would bark back a hello if she wasn't on the job. And she was on the job more than she was off. She knew right now that I was on my own, so she felt obligated to get me home safely before she could do normal dog stuff.

Just as I began to truly appreciate the walk, we were home. Sherpa turned me up my own sidewalk.

I walked in and found Patrick playing a video game in the living room. I walked around the couch and listened a bit as his character racked up a bunch of skill points by doing tricks. I think it was a skateboarding game.

"Hey," I said.

"Hey," he replied, a bit of caution in his voice.

"You wanna go to Jack's and grab a late lunch? It sounded busy when I walked by, but I bet it clears out soon once the next round of games starts in the park."

I heard him pause the game and toss the controller to the floor. "Are you serious?"

"Yeah. Why?"

"You have never invited me to do anything with you ever."

"That can't be true. We've done all kinds of things together." I was sure of it.

"We have," he agreed, "but always initiated by me. You're seriously asking me to spend time with you?" His voice cracked, and I could tell he was close to tears.

"Okay, okay, let's not turn to mush about it," I begged. "I'm hungry, I thought maybe you'd be hungry. We don't have to make this a Dr. Phil situation."

"Good, cause I was faking anyway," he sneered, standing up. "Let's go, lame brain. You're buying!"

He zipped out the door and left Sherpa and I to walk all on our own. He was on the bench outside the restaurant when I arrived.

"Took you long enough."

⚡

"Here are your breadsticks," the waitress said as she laid the tray on the table. Her name was Kelly, and I'd been waited on by her before. She seemed a little quieter than normal today, but I chalked it up to the busy lunch rush.

We'd ordered my usual appetizer, the nacho breadsticks—zesty breadsticks seasoned and oiled, served with nacho cheese dipping sauce. Henry had once declared they could be used in church as the body and blood of Christ during communion, they were so tasty. But Henry said that would probably be sacrilegious so we never brought it up with any clergy members or church folk. He had been right about the deliciousness, though.

"So how are you doing?" I offered, trying to connect with my younger brother for once. I'd had plenty of opportunities to protect him and be an older brother physically . . . but I was suddenly distressed realizing how little time I'd spent trying to actually get to know the kid.

He answered in between bites. "I don't know. I guess okay. You meet Dad's new girlfriend?"

"Yeah," I replied. "She seems nice, I guess."

"I thought he'd end up dating someone a lot more like Mom," Pat noted. "But she does seem nice, and he seems happy."

"Yeah," I agreed before chomping on a bite of cheese-dipped garlic bread. "Holy sh—" I caught myself before I finished the swear but spit out the breadstick. "That is way too hot!"

Patrick laughed a bit, like little brothers do when they think they've scored some kind of life points against their older sibling. Then he bit boldly into a breadstick of his own and had a little pot calling the kettle situation as he sucked down cola to drench the heat.

"Do you ever think about Mom?" Suddenly I was using this rare brotherly lunch for my own mental health exploration.

"Sometimes, I guess," Patrick allowed. "Man this nacho cheese is spicy!"

"Did you already drain your drink?" I raised my hand for the waitress to return as Patrick dealt with a burnt tongue and a runny nose.

"Thanks," Pat said to Kelly after she'd refilled the drinks and given us extra napkins.

"Let's get back to Mom. What do you remember about her? When you think about her . . . what are you picturing?"

Pat continued eating the breadsticks and spicy cheese dip, even as he tried to answer the question. "I was eleven when you were twelve. You remember her death because you were there. All I remember is going to bed with a mom and waking up without one. And it's still the worst day of my life." He was so casual in tone, but the words were brutal.

If I was honest, I'd never given much thought to Patrick's reaction and experience after Mom's death. I'd been so fixated on my own. Selfish yet again. My biggest sin was selfishness.

I was good at being selfish. It suited me, and I hated it.

Patrick may have even had it rougher than I did, being just young enough to not be able to process but old enough to know the finality of it all.

The pizza finally arrived, giving both of us a chance to say nothing and process the discussion we'd had thus far as we stuffed our faces.

Even after expanding to Goodspeed, Jack's quality never waned. There is something comforting in absolutely knowing without a doubt that the food you are about to eat will be tremendous. We spent a good four to six minutes munching and groaning.

After two pieces, I was ready for a break in the eating.

"Are those really the only details about Mom's death that you remember?"

"Yes."

"Do you want me to give you more specific information about that event?"

"Yes."

"Are you sure?"

"I don't know, man," he said. "You're the one who has the details. I don't. So . . . do I want to know them?"

I really don't think you do.

"I'm not sure, buddy. I really don't know," I said.

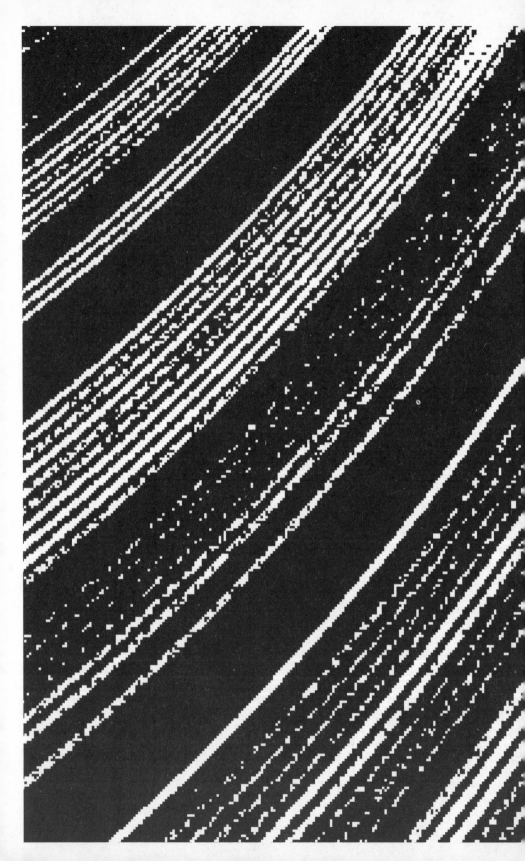

9

THE WINDY CITY

Date night in Chicago was winding down. Emmaline and I had enjoyed a lovely Italian meal. The girl loved pasta more than anything. She just loved it. I have no idea where she put it, since she was skinnier than me.

After dinner we went to a movie—the latest slapstick comedy from a guy named Toby Norman. Everyone acted like they hated his brand of comedy whenever it was being discussed in public, but all his movies made tons of money. I thought it was an interesting phenomenon.

I decided to try using one of those audio description headsets for the visually impaired. It's literally having a voice in your headphones describe to you everything that happens. I have to say, it's a lovely, romantic idea and I applaud its very existence. But it's also not like truly watching a movie. Despite its good intentions, it's ultimately not very practical.

"The character is dancing while intoxicated." "The glass breaks in a humorous fashion." "She makes an 'Oh no you didn't' face."

Movies are a lot less exciting when they are explained to you in this manner. On top of that, the descriptions talked over the actual movie's dialogue and other audio that would be important to the overall experience. So when the headphones were telling me the protagonist had swapped the villain's gun for a prop gun, I couldn't hear whatever the villain was saying, which turned out to be crucial plot information—as much as any plot information in a comedy can be considered crucial.

Imagine your favorite song comes on the radio, but instead of being able to hear it the DJ keeps talking over it about his favorite parts and the notable instrumental section. You'd change the station, which is basically what I did too.

About thirty minutes into the film I gave up on the headphones and decided to just absorb the film with my ears, old-fashioned style. The added bonus was it was easier to hear Emm's giggling without the headphones. It was a good sound . . . a comforting sound.

When the film ended, we sat in our seats as the credits rolled and the other patrons filed out. It was just easier for us to navigate public spaces when there were fewer people.

We walked down the stairs of the cinema's main entrance to the sidewalk and a bustling downtown Chicago. Even in September it was still a windy city, just not a cold one quite yet. If you've never walked along Michigan Avenue in the dead of winter with high lake winds whipping against you, I'm not sure you've truly known cold.

"What did you think of the movie?" I asked. Typically in situations like this, we'd head for an isolated place where no one might see us disappear when we teleported back to Freepoint. This could be a park or an alley, sometimes a closet or elevator. Tonight it seemed more like we were walking aimlessly with no real destination in mind, which was fine with me.

I would follow her anywhere.

"It was so funny," she laughed, talking about the movie.

Emmaline usually led the way when we walked. She had vision and I did not; it just made sense. She led when we walked, she led when we danced. She led when we spent three years transitioning from good friends to dating partners. She led the way for me in morality, empathy, and forgiveness. I admired so many qualities about her that, at times, it was difficult to see why someone like her would have an interest in someone like me.

"Was it better than his last one?" I asked.

"The one with the dancing seals? Oh, god no!" She cackled a bit louder, fondly remembering the dancing seals. "That's still the best Toby Norman movie ever, even better than *Santasplosion*, and you know how much I love that one."

"I do." *Santasplosion* was, in fact, terrible. The premise was that Santa entered a cloning machine just before a power surge, resulting in over a million Santas out there trying to do the job and be the guy, watering down the very notion of Santa Claus and, indeed, Christmas spirit itself. The *Nashville Times* newspaper called it "a shameless excuse of a film made only to pad the lead actor's bank account."

"But this one was solid. Top half of his movies, I think." She wound down her amateur review. "I'd watch it again, that's for sure."

"Me too," I joked.

"I guess the headphones didn't help much?" Emm had been suggesting I try the descriptive audio stuff for a while now, and she sounded sad that they hadn't worked out. I hated to give her bad news.

"It's just too much talking. Too many words. They describe everything— the actions of the characters, the background, the weather. They end up talking all over the actual dialogue and explosions and other movie audio that makes a movie exciting."

She sighed. "Sorry it didn't work out. I was really hoping it would add to the experience for you, not take away from it."

"Eh, I just need eyes," I said sarcastically.

She squeezed my hand. "You heard what your dad said last week. The scientists are getting really close. It's going to happen eventually, P."

"Yeah," I concurred. "Then I'll get sight, but I'll also be able to feel guilty about all the other Ables whose disabilities science hasn't cured yet."

Science was definitely going to cure blindness soon, and hearing loss. Weak organs, sluggish cells—all fixable. But many disabilities were not reversible by scientific discovery. Those individuals would always be disabled, perhaps even more marginalized by society *after* fake eyes and fake ears solved a lot of disabled peoples' problems.

I could hear her shaking her head back and forth, mostly because of the wind patterns as she moved, tiny strands of audio slipping between her strands of hair. "You don't have to see every glass as half empty," she reminded me, for maybe the three hundredth time. "It's okay to celebrate your victories, even if they are unique to you."

"I'd be able to see the glass as half full if I could at least see the glass itself." It was a line I'd used before, and it represented to Emmaline my desire not to continue this line of discussion.

She let go of my hand and breathed, "Semantics."

You idiot, I told myself silently. *You do this every single time. Why are you so stubborn?*

My therapist thought it was about control. I felt safer and happier the more control I had over a situation or event. The less control I had or felt, the more my anxiety and panic escalated. And if and when my girlfriend was making more sense than me, winning an argument . . . it made me feel a lack of control.

But a necessary one.

"You're right," I finally sighed. Those were the two hardest words for me to say to anyone who wasn't me. You're right—and I'm not. Ugh. What bile. "I'm still defaulting to pessimism . . . skepticism . . . nay-saying. I don't want to be, but I am."

"I know there are some terrible memories in there." She finger-tapped my right temple playfully. "But there are good ones too. I was there for some of them. You just need to give the good memories as much airtime as you give the negative ones." She grabbed my hand again.

I wanted to push back at that last statement. That was my nature.

I also thought the bad memories deserved more airtime so we wouldn't forget and make the same mistakes twice. Mom's death. James's death. Henry's death. All retraceable to my specific actions or decisions. No single villain put behind bars could ever measure up to the pulsing pain felt by the remaining family members of a dead custodian.

I realized then that I'd lost track of our steps and our turns, and therefore our location. It usually didn't take Emm this long to find a private spot to teleport from, even in a city the size of Chicago.

"Where are we?" I wondered aloud.

Emmaline laughed a bit. "Exactly how daring are you feeling?" she asked.

"Like . . . on a scale of one to ten?"

"Sure."

"I think I'm probably always resting around a four or a five. I'm not a daring kind of person, you see," I fumbled. "But I suppose I could be persuaded to be more daring if there were a good reason." I paused. "Is there a good reason?"

"I don't want to teleport home. At least not from here." Her voice sounded flat, calm, and full of warmth.

These days I teleported a lot of places—university, team practice, custodial missions—and it was all because of Emmaline. And it was always a matter of common sense. Like when we planned this date night, we didn't plan any time for travel, mostly because Chicago was almost two hours from Freepoint by car. It was assumed we would teleport. And with that assumption came an assumed obligation for Emmaline, which I hadn't ever really thought much about.

It just made sense and saved time to teleport.

"I want to ride the train," she said, as though confessing a guilty pleasure.

"You do?" I'd ridden on the trains in Chicago, and they were as worthy of mockery as the trains in DC and New York. Don't even get me started on the ancient twisty underground cars in Boston. It was my official opinion that subway trains were the worst.

"I've never been on one," she explained. "I know people make jokes about them, but how bad can they be? Ever since I've been able to teleport, I've teleported. And before that, we lived in Indiana in a town of three thousand farmers! I've never even been on an airplane!"

I cringed slightly. "I've had some rough flights myself." I shook my head. "I can't, in good conscience, recommend airplanes to you."

"I'm just saying I want to experience normal life a bit! I want to take the long way!" She was so excited it was hard to keep from smiling right along with her.

I tried to put my therapy to use and empathize with Emmaline's position. Sure, the subways were dirty and hot and awful to anyone like me who had ever been on them.

But Emm hadn't been on them. She'd been teleporting instantly everywhere she went since she was twelve. New experiences, even if they come with grime or dirt or regret, can still be entertaining for those new to the event. Like a child's first time stomping in a rain puddle—messy for sure, but totally worth the experience.

"Okay, okay," I offered. "We can take a train. But the farthest station out toward home still leaves us with seventy-eight miles to traverse after the last subway station."

She reached up and hooked her hand inside my elbow. "We can rent a car!"

"Alright," I laughed. "But you should know that I'm a terrible driver."

"And I don't have a license!" she added.

We both laughed for a few seconds.

"I'll just teleport us home from the last station," she announced. "It's not about not teleporting, it's about experiencing the trains!"

"Alright, let's do it," I agreed. "I do hope you realize I have no idea which way the nearest subway station is and so you'll have to lead us to our destination."

"What do you think I've been doing the last few minutes," she asked playfully.

$$\frac{1}{2}$$

After a bit of frustration with the automated kiosk, we finally caught the Blue Line downtown and were headed west out toward O'Hare Airport.

From there Emm could pop us home instantly after she had her fun experiencing an authentic Chicago subway ride—or so I hoped.

I knew this train line had sections that were elevated and other subterranean sections as well, so it would offer the full scope of the Chicago train experience.

When we boarded the train car, it was half full, mostly with normal-sounding people. Everyone seemed exhausted, bored, and anxious. "So many heads buried in so many phones," Emm said. A few people were even sleeping; imagine being that trusting or that tired, that you would literally fall asleep on a public train and hope no one robbed you or beat you up or otherwise messed with you.

The car lurched forward, filling my nose and lungs with the smell of subway air. It was equal parts coffee, alcohol, sweat, perfume, and curry.

At first, Emmaline was loving it. "This is so authentic!" she whispered excitedly into my ear. "It's real Chicago! Real transportation!"

Emmaline looked for seat belts for a good ten seconds before giving up.

I didn't want to rob her of her first subway car experience, so I was mostly just observing with my nonvisual senses as she went through things herself for the first time. The trains in Chicago could be quite lurchy, even if one was used to subway cars from other cities.

Some men nearby were talking about their business meeting. I was thrilled to hear an out-of-tune violin as the train got moving, suggesting at least one subway musician was on board. Honestly, the musicians on the trains and in the stations are half of what makes the subway tolerable.

The train lurched suddenly around a tight corner.

Emmaline made a noise; it sounded like a groan. I wasn't sure if I should even mention it at all or just let it go. I decided to play it safe and just said, "Um . . ."

There was no response.

We reached the next stop. The violin player exited, and a few new riders got on. From the sound of it, they were all standing and grabbing the overhead handles.

They seemed to be college kids, mostly talking about classes and assignments and campus rules and such.

The business guys had gotten off the train without my ever learning what kind of business they were in, which bothered me greatly. It might have been the steel business, or the leather clothing business, or even the electric car business . . . but they were all gonna make tons of money, and I now had no inkling as to how.

I felt Emmaline lean in closer, and then I heard her soft words on my ears. "This is so much fun. Thank you." Some kids are so sheltered by overprotective parents that even the most mundane public activity can be a healing salve.

Oddly, despite my blindness, I was far more comfortable in this situation than she was, purely due to experience. I'd ridden trains most of my early youth growing up in New York City, but to her a subway car was as foreign as a space shuttle.

Just then we rounded a sudden sharp curve, and Emmaline lost her balance. I threw my arms out to try and help, but I didn't know exactly where she was, so I missed.

It was too late anyway. Emmaline's disability caused her to fall down or pass out in times when her equilibrium got confused. And she'd hit the floor of the subway car before I'd even fully realized anything had gone wrong.

But I didn't have time to spend on that, as the college kids at the far end of the train had also been observing things and chose this as their moment to move in and intimidate me.

"Hey there," I heard one of them say.

"Yo," another called in my direction.

"Just stay right there, son" the other one chimed in. "We can help," he added, unconvincingly. They must have noticed my cane and presumed my blindness.

Do I have an uncanny knack for running into bad people, or are, like, half the people in the world just bad people?

"Is she okay?" another voice asked. His words were harmless, but his tone was a mocking one.

The car had gotten fairly empty without me realizing it, mostly because I was too busy thinking about Emmaline and being a doofus.

Suddenly, the entire car lurched to a stop. For a moment everything went quiet. I heard a few faint popping noises.

Oh no, I thought. *Not right now.*

My teleporting girlfriend had collapsed and was currently unconscious, the power just went out, and four or five drunk fraternity hoodlums were about to assault me just for laughs and not for any reasonable objective or purpose.

Wonderful.

10

THE TRAIN

The lack of electricity did nothing to slow my would-be attackers. The four thugs inched closer, intent on mocking me as they approached. My hearing was working fine, of course, so they had less of an advantage than they believed.

I was sure there were four of them now, not five.

I considered my options. I could definitely just send out a wide telekinetic blast, and the force would take them all out. But that method would also probably result in serious injury to one of them, or even death.

"Mr. Magoo!" one called out.

"Hey," another called. "Which hand am I holding my brass knuckles in?"

A different one joined in the mockery. "Which hand am I holding a knife in?"

Yet another cackled, "The soup of the day is blind guy puree!"

I positioned myself between Emmaline and the attackers and dropped my cane to the ground.

"Uh oh," the one nearest me mock-cried. "Looks like he's getting serious, guys." I could tell from the direction of his voice that he was about ten feet in front of me, and two inches shorter than me. But he was confident. He had the numbers, his sole opponent was blind, and he had no idea I was a custodian. Why should he?

"This is gonna be fun," sneered the farthest one back. He was maybe twenty-two feet away, but definitely taller than me by a good bit.

"Nah," countered the thug about seventeen feet away, and off to the left. "It'll be over too quick to be any fun, I bet."

These guys are good. This is like a routine they've practiced or something. I turned my body ninety degrees so my left side faced the oncoming bullies, while slipping my right hand into my pocket to grab the clicker.

"Now he means business for sure," the fourth one cackled. He was off to the right side of the car, about the same distance as voice three. The four of them formed a diamond. "Is that karate?"

"It's ear karate! He's kung fu listening!"

I turned the clicker in my fingers so that it was pointed at my attackers, then swept my left ear left to right to get a clean read of the train car.

The nearest guy laughed. "Are your ears gonna save you, kid?"

"Yes," I said just above a whisper.

I flipped the clicker into rapid mode and pressed the button. In less than a second it fired off three dozen bursts in a spread formation, echoing and returning back to my ears almost instantly. It wouldn't last long, but now I had a tighter read on everyone's position and stance.

"The hell—" the lead jerk started. But it was already too late.

I squared up to them and brought my wrists together, hands open, and hit the main bad guy square in the chest with the force of a solid linebacker tackle in college football. He was thrown back several feet, flat on his back as he slid even farther.

I fluidly crossed my arms and "felt" around for the two midrange bullies' shirt collars. I locked in pretty quickly, since they were busy gaping at their groaning buddy on the ground. Then I simply uncrossed my arms violently and rapidly, slamming each of them into the opposite wall of the train.

Might have broken a couple bones there, I admitted silently.

Suddenly my leg started screaming at me, and I felt a strange sensation I'd never experienced before.

What is that? I don't think that's . . . I reached down to find the handle of a knife sticking out of my right thigh. It was sticky with blood.

I briefly considered sending the knife right back at the tall one in the back who'd thrown it, but I had been doing well lately on my promise to Dad to be less violent. Apparently there's only so many times you're allowed to get away with it by saying "He doesn't know his own strength." After a while . . . he knows it, and you know he knows it.

Instead, I remembered something I'd heard in a movie once: that if you pull out a knife the wound will just bleed more rapidly. So I left the knife where it was and just screamed.

"Ahhhhhhh! You stabbed me!"

"I just threw the knife, man," he replied meekly.

"You threw a knife at a blind kid," I bellowed.

"You messed up my friends," he defended. I could hear that he was backing away from me as much as he could and was pressed almost up against the train car's rear door.

"Whatever, man," I sighed angrily. "Picking on a blind kid and his passed out girlfriend." I knelt down and tried to rouse Emmaline, but she was still out. I moved my fingers to check her pulse, not because I thought she was dead but because I wanted to get a feel for her heartbeat.

"What are you, one of those janitor freaks?" he yelled, a cornered dog giving off some courage barks.

The train's rear door had a large piece of Plexiglas window in the center, the kind I knew would pop out rather than shattering and cutting the guy. So I just lifted my left arm and blasted him through it and onto the track.

Now how the heck am I going to get us out of here?

Now that the train's back window had been blown out, I could hear that we were in one of the aboveground areas of the Blue Line's track. We weren't far from the airport; I could hear a couple dozen airliners circling not far overhead. With no power on the ground at the airport, the planes couldn't land. They'd circle for a while and, if necessary, eventually divert to another nearby city's airport.

Good, we're above ground. If we had been underground in one of the tunnels, I don't know what I would have done.

I heard groans coming from the three thugs still on the train car as they stirred. I reached out mentally, searching for the handle on the back door of the train. It took only a quick moment. I turned the handle from twenty-five feet away, and the door swung open.

"Get out of here," I said to them.

They were smart enough to want to avoid any more fighting, so they scampered to their feet and ran away.

I picked up my cane and folded it up, sliding it into my pocket.

"Okay, Emm," I said, leaning down over her. "Let's get you up."

I reached my arms under her frame and lifted with my knees, standing to my feet. My skinny arms were probably just barely strong enough to carry her, but I used my powers to supplement my muscles. I'd always been skinny and slight, and it was tough to get motivated to lift weights or bulk up when my particular abilities far outranked muscle strength anyway.

I walked through the now empty train car to the doorway. I heard sirens all over the place, and lots of cars and trucks.

I'd momentarily forgotten about the knife in my leg, but the last few steps to the doorway were a sharp reminder.

I assessed my options. I couldn't walk while carrying Emmaline for very long with this knife wound in my leg. Enough people were on the roads, either fleeing the blackout or trying to get home to family, a ride service home would be impossible. The flights were grounded, none of my Ables friends were here or would be able to find us to save us, the cell phones wouldn't work, and my teleporting girlfriend was unconscious.

I'm going to have to fly home, I realized.

I tried rattling off a list of concerns: circling airliners, local small planes and helicopters, tall buildings and trees, drones, hills, and other elevation changes. Blindness.

I did have an excellent sense of direction. And I knew where O'Hare Airport was in relation to downtown and in relation to my town. Freepoint was basically southwest of the airport, about seventy or eighty miles. I was pretty confident I could get close on the direction.

The more challenging trick would be finding the right altitude. I'd have to be high enough not to smack into a high-rise apartment building or cell phone tower, but low enough to avoid aircraft.

It was a good bet the passenger and cargo jets would be at high enough elevations for me to avoid easily.

Helicopters could technically fly at any altitude, but typically they stayed at heights above the tall buildings downtown. I figured two thousand feet.

Personal airplanes, little two-seaters and such, would be even higher than that.

So what's the tallest thing between here and home that's under two thousand feet?

Bentley would have been so handy right now.

Oh yeah, electric cables! This is going to be so impossible.

I figured I'd start simple and fly straight up, maybe to one hundred feet or so. And then I could get a sense of things from there before making my next move.

I should have known better. I should have realized I'd forgotten some important detail or possible danger—like the concrete interstate overpass that was fifty feet directly above my head.

"One hundred feet, nice and slow," I said as I lifted off the ground with Emm in my arms.

Except that even if you're going nice and slow, running into an unexpected object can still hurt like hell, and this did. My body went limp as the top of my head smacked the concrete, Emmaline falling from my grasp instantly.

Now, I'm not positive how long it takes a person to fall fifty feet, but it's not a very long time. Thankfully it was just enough time for me to shake free of the bell-ringing effects in my skull, realize I'd dropped my girlfriend, reach out mentally with my abilities to find her, focus on that intensely enough to grab hold of her wrists, and stop her fall. I'm guessing it was 2.7 seconds.

I pulled her up to me with little effort and hugged her as I held her again in my arms. *I am never telling her about this*, I told myself.

Before anyone else nearly died at my hands tonight, I thought it might be best to head back to solid ground and think of a new plan, maybe even wait out the power outage—though in New York, the outage had taken days to be repaired. If this citywide outage was related, we could be here a while.

I started descending back to the roof of the train, not going fast or anything, but not exactly moving slowly. If I'd been moving more slowly . . . well . . . we may never know.

But this is when Emmaline woke up—while *falling* through the air in a pitch-black scene. Her head had been tilted away from me, so her first view didn't tell her anything good about the present situation.

A few days later I would learn that Emmaline had a bit of a custodial tick. When her fight-or-flight response started misfiring or overfiring, she would teleport back to her safe place—not on purpose or even with her input. It was more of a reflex, like when the doctor hammers your knee.

Emmaline's current safe place was her bedroom in her parents' home in Freepoint.

And this is how Emm and I found ourselves popping into her bedroom near the ceiling, continuing our descent I'd begun back before she woke up, and crashing onto her bed together. Some part of the wooden frame made a snapping noise, and a picture fell off the wall on top of the two of us.

I took a few deep breaths and then slowly groaned, "What in the hell just happened?"

"That's what I'd like to know," said a male voice from the doorway.

"Daddy," Emmaline said, "it's not what it looks like."

RESEARCH

Thursday evening was usually a night most of the Ables crew got together out at Charles Field. Sometimes we'd run drills and practice to stay sharp as heroes. Sometimes we trained for the university version of the SuperSim games. And sometimes we just played games or hung out and talked.

Whenever it rained, we went to Bentley's house. Bentley's father was on the run from the law, still wanted for his role in the puppet-master events in Washington DC. Both the United States court system and a custodial council awarded Bentley and his mother the entire family estate, which included the mansion in Freepoint and more money than they'd ever be able to count or spend.

All of Bentley's brothers were older and off with their own families now, so there was plenty of room at the Crittendon house.

Traditionally, Bentley kept an eye on the weather forecast and would send everyone a message if we were looking at a rainout, so we'd all know to head to his place. And tonight he had not sent such a text—but it was pouring. Even without a mass message, most everyone showed up at Bentley's house at six thirty.

We were greeted at the door by Olivia, Bentley's former nanny, who'd remained with the family as the housekeeper and chef. We'd all known her for years.

"Welcome, welcome," she said when Emmaline and I walked in. I was walking better already, even just a few days after the knife wound. Turns out it had missed most of the crucial muscles. I was able to get around pretty well with a cane, and a week later I was walking on my own.

"Hey, Olivia," Emm said with a smile in her voice.

"How's Abby?" I asked.

"She's good, she's good. She's at piano practice, but she'll be home in a bit."

One by one we showed up. Emmaline and I. Greta. Echo. Freddie and Lacene arrived a few seconds before Luc. Lead Foot came with Patrick and their new friend Neddy. Finally Penelope arrived. We all stood there in the foyer for several minutes, mostly chatting and catching up.

"Is Bentley here?" I asked Penelope, wondering what was taking so long.

"I thought so," she said.

Eventually Mrs. Crittendon walked in. She sounded tired even as she also sounded happy to see us. "Oh, hello, guys! What are you all doing here in the foyer? Go on up there. He's in the lab. You know the way. Good to see you all!"

Now, you might be wondering why we allowed something like rain to drive our get-togethers indoors when Penelope's powers allowed her to control the weather. But Penelope had a strict rule about her abilities; she never wanted to use them selfishly or unnaturally, only for strategic or battle reasons. If it was raining right now, her view was that it was supposed to be raining, and she wasn't going to get in the way of the natural order of things. Though I was frustrated occasionally that we couldn't practice when we needed to, I mostly respected her stance. There weren't enough people taking a stance these days.

Bentley's house was a mansion. It was a good two-minute walk from the downstairs foyer to his upstairs lab. Because the great staircase was circular and spanned the walls of the entire great room, there were fifty-eight steps to the top.

The second floor had once been the palace of Jurrious (Bentley's dad), and Bentley'd had the third floor for his bedroom and lab. But a couple years ago Bentley moved down a floor and made his father's former office into his own office/laboratory.

When we reached the end of the hallway, the door to the lab was open, but we didn't hear anything inside the room.

"Hello? Bent?" I called out as I ventured in first.

Everyone followed me in, and we kind of milled about murmuring. The sighted kids were all checking out the shelves and books and machines. Glass cases were everywhere, each housing something old or new but precious nonetheless.

Greta gushed over a "gnarly" sword hanging on the wall.

Neddy and Patrick thought they spotted a prototype for a time machine.

"I didn't realize it would be so dark in here," Emm said.

"I'm sure he's got lights that aren't turned on right now," I replied.

I heard a faint, distant snap. I shook it off as nothing.

Luc had found Bentley's own EMP invention. Being one whose superpower was that he was an EMP, Luc got excited a bit. I heard some of the others laughing, enjoying his happiness.

There was another tiny cracking noise in the background. This time I turned to the left, from where it had come. "Emm?" I pointed. "What's over here? A wall? A door?"

"Haven't you been over here a bunch?" she asked, surprised.

"Not in here, no. His old lab upstairs, yeah . . . but not this one." The sadness in my voice was obvious, as I couldn't hide my disappointment at the current lack of a closeness with Bentley that used to be there.

"Sorry," she said. "All bookshelves floor to ceiling on that wall except a single door."

Just then there were enough zapping noises, loud ones, that everyone in the lab turned toward the sound. The room shook slightly, like a mild earthquake. Emm later said she could even see a faint flickering blue light along the edge of the doorframe.

And then . . . nothing. Silence.

Then the door opened. Bentley stepped out briskly, closed the door, and noticed all of us standing there. "Oh good," he said. "You're here!"

He walked through the group, whistling along as he made his way to the far wall and his workbench, as though he'd been expecting us just now and that none of this was the least bit strange.

"Bentley, what's in there?" I pointed at the wall of bookshelves and the door he'd just come out of.

"That? That's my secret lab. This here"—he paused, likely to gesture—"is my main lab."

"Okay, but what's with all the racket in there a second ago?" I prodded further.

"Nothing. Nothing important. That's the room where I work on the machines that are failures, and this is the room where I'm proud enough of what I've done to store or work on it in here. Like this." I heard the sound of metal and leather hit the workshop table.

For a few beats, no one said anything.

"Looks like a strap with a clasp," Patrick finally offered. "Big whoop. You invented the belt."

"It is a strap, Patty, it is!" Bentley was really excited about this thing and just kept on going. Patrick never really got an open window to yell at him for using the forbidden nickname. "More appropriately, it's a harness—a harness to help Phillip and Emmaline fight even more streamlined! Come here, come here, come here," he repeated to the two of us. We walked over to where he was standing.

Bentley then proceeded to act like he didn't know I was blind as he showed the device off to everyone else in the room. "So this here, goes here. And this . . . goes here. Then . . . connect the strap, ticktock, there you go!"

And everyone around me ooh'd and aah'd. When the appreciation subsided, I cleared my throat in that obnoxious way one does to get attention.

"Emmaline?" I heard Bentley say.

Emmaline then walked the few steps toward me and silently attached the device to my right arm. I felt her lay her own right arm underneath mine as she stood in front with her back to me. A strap tightened around our arms together.

"Now imagine," she said softly, "instead of vertical, horizontal, type of force, and strength . . . I only have to call out type and strength." Then, moving her arm to the right and up a few degrees, which brought my own strapped-in arm along the same trajectory, she said, "Push, 50 percent."

"But don't actually do that!" Bentley immediately begged.

"Holy shit," Freddie breathed aloud.

"That's amazing," Patrick followed immediately.

I just shook my head in wonder, even though I should have long ago stopped being surprised by Bentley's genius.

"I know it seems like a small thing, but it's 50 percent of your entire battle language," Bentley explained.

"No," I admitted, "I get it." I was impressed.

He continued as though he hadn't heard me. "In real time out in the field, it's going to make you guys twice as efficient—which is a little frightening, but hey, we are living in frightening times, right? Maybe we need something to frighten those who frighten us."

"Speaking of," I said, anxious to see if Bentley had learned anything about the blackouts, "turn up anything yet?"

"Yes and no," he answered, and then he was off again, walking toward the corner of the room. Emm told me that on the wall was a massive hyperthin monitor screen, connected to pretty much all of Bentley's computers and probably a video game system or six.

I heard him punch some keys on a keyboard, and then he proceeded to walk us all through the images on the giant screen.

"These power outages are interesting for a few reasons," he began. "To begin with, they weren't power failures, as we typically know them. Power failures are when a connection or two is severed and large swaths of customers stop receiving power. In these two instances in New York and Chicago, that's not what happened." His voice shook with excitement. It was obvious he couldn't wait to share what it was that he had found.

"You have to be my eyes, Emm," I said, for maybe the hundredth time since I'd met her.

"Of course," she replied, as she always did.

"This outage worked from the outside in," Bentley declared.

Emm whispered, "He has a graphic showing the outage starting from the outside and moving inward. It's pretty cool, if I'm honest," she added.

"So what does that mean?" Patrick asked before I had a chance.

"Good question!" Bentley exclaimed. "It means that whoever or whatever stole all that electricity was in the center of the grid when they did it."

"Wait," I blurted out. "You think someone stole that electricity? You're saying this isn't just a couple of blackouts?"

"That's correct," he replied, clearly still smiling. "Electricity has to go somewhere, friends. It cannot simply disappear. That's not how science works. In a blackout, sure, the power goes out to the affected areas, but only because of a severed conduit. The station still holds on to the electricity, it just can't deliver it to customers. This? This was different."

Freddy chimed in. "It might be time to switch to decaf, Bentley."

"No," Greta countered. "I was just reading about this. He's right. Electricity is matter. It can't just disappear!"

"Correct!" Bentley was like a professor, giddy to have students who understood the material. "Greta gets the gold star."

"So if the electricity was sucked inward, then in order to find out who or what stole it, we need to find the mathematical center of each blackout?" I asked, trying to keep us on task.

"Already done," Bentley replied. "I analyzed the data from both blackouts and pinpointed the center—the spot where all the electricity flowed." He punched some keys on one of the computers.

"He's got side-by-side graphics of each city's blackout center," Emm whispered, keeping me visually in the loop.

"Then I tapped into a few satellites and accessed surveillance cameras from businesses in those areas, and only one face was found in both cities' blackout centers." Another keystroke. "This man."

Emm described the image. "Long blond hair, strong features."

"Who is he?" I asked, voicing what we were all wondering.

"No clue," Bentley declared.

"What?" I wasn't accustomed to Bentley saying he didn't know. It was a very rare occurrence. And he'd identified targets before from a single photo, so I knew he had some databases he could search.

"He's not in any system I have access to. That means he's not in the databases for the FBI, the DHS, Interpol, TSA . . . he's a ghost."

"Great," I sighed dejectedly.

"So we're back at square one?" Luc asked.

"Not entirely," Bentley replied, giving us some hope. "The tricky part will be running the facial recognition software to find a match."

"A match?" Lacene inquired.

Bentley explained, "Even if he's not in any database we can search, we know he's real. He's a person. He's standing right there! All we have to do is find him."

"And you can do that with facial recognition software?" Greta asked.

"Sure." He sounded so casual and confident. "All we have to do is search surveillance video from . . . well . . . all over the world. And if he's shown his face in public, eventually we'll find him."

"Isn't that illegal?" Emmaline asked. "Didn't the government outlaw facial recognition software?"

"Yeah," Bentley confirmed, "for humans."

"Wait," Freddie started. "Are you breaking the law with this stuff?"

"Eh, law shmlaw," Bentley retorted. "It's all a gray area anyway. If I'm able to spot bad guys early or help us fine-tune our heroism, what's the harm done?"

"Look," I started to object, "I'm all for catching this guy, but I'm not sure I want to blur the legal lines as much as you do. Facial recognition software has been banned in the US for several years now."

"Because they can't use it ethically, because there were thousands of people with access, ensuring a certain percentage of them were of ill intent," he argued. "It went from cops using it to catch bad guys to pop stars using it to better target merchandise sales to concertgoers. Too many with access is what poisoned the technology."

"Whereas now we have just one?" I asked with a dose of sarcasm. "You're the decider on if this guy is worth using illegal technology to find? Last time I checked, Bentley, we were a team, man. You and Henry and I . . . we used to make decisions together!"

"Used to," Bentley spat. "Henry's gone now. So if I know you won't agree with me, what's the point in taking a vote or even asking?"

"You guys!" Freddie yelled, shaking us from our stupor. "You can have this argument later, but right now we are trying to figure out who is behind the blackouts!"

I took a deep breath, and it sounded like Bentley did as well. We wanted the same thing, and we both seemed to realize it in that moment.

"Do it," I said. "Use the software."

"I'm sorry," Bentley added, sounding both mad at me yet also apologetic for the barb about Henry.

There were cameras all over every major US city. Some had more than others. Chicago was particularly high on the surveillance cam list, but only because it was just as high on the crime-death-fear list.

Bentley had spotted a male figure near the center of the power outage—which he really wanted us to start calling "The Suckage"—and he thought he could run an algorithm to search for any other surveillance or satellite image around the globe that might be a match. Find a match, and we'd have a starting place for narrowing our search.

He typed for several seconds before dramatically hitting one key with great vigor.

"Okay," he sighed.

"Well," I asked aloud, "what did you learn?"

"Oh," he replied, a sheepish grin in his voice. "I only just now told the computer to start running the calculation. Ha ha ha. Oh, misunderstanding here! I mean, it could take weeks for this equation to be worked out! Do you have any idea how many satellite images we have to sort through?"

So we are back to square one, I assumed.

12

PROJECTING

That night my vivid dreams returned.

I was standing on one of those people-mover things, like you find in airports. It's an escalator, but instead of stairs it's flat, so people weary of walking can just stand for a few seconds and still make progress toward their gate.

I was the only person on the contraption going in my direction, but the opposite side, headed the other way, was full of people.

I checked my boarding pass to see if I was going the right direction, and it read "Yes, you are supposed to be alone."

Soon, among the travelers on the opposite-facing people mover, I began to see some faces that I recognized.

First came James. "Watch your step," he said cheerily. "Don't fall." He handed me a business card and then glided on by.

I flipped the card over and it said "James Was Here."

If you're wondering about the visual details in this account, I can tell you that in many of my dreams I am not blind. I have no idea if other blind people have the same experiences or if this just happens to me because, for a time, I *did* have sight . . . but many of my dreams were visually vivid.

As the belt continued pushing me forward, I looked down and saw that I had cinder blocks for feet. The me in the dream laughed about it, then

91

looked up to see my mother pass by on the other belt. "I'm happy to have died saving you, son." She smiled as she passed by. "You were worth it."

I checked my boarding pass again, certain I was going the wrong direction. Now it read "You already asked me that." I looked up again at the other conveyor belt.

Along came Henry, standing with no wheelchair, arms crossed defiantly. "Can you guess what I'm thinking?" he called as he slid by. "Go ahead," he said and smiled, "read my mind."

Some more strangers passed, and then Patrick appeared, with Sherpa on a leash with him. "I'll take good care of her, man," he said, smiling.

And that's when I woke up, drenched in sweat, panting for air, and shaking my head.

This is getting worse.

"What do you think you've learned from this experience on the train?" my therapist asked. "Do you feel like you changed at all as a result of the events?"

"I mean . . ." I started, stammering, "I failed, again. I failed as soon as I started."

"Let's talk about that," she said. I swear to God the first course in being a shrink is called Let's Talk About That 101. "You say you failed. I'm assuming you mean hitting your head on the bridge, correct?"

"Correct."

"But why do you gloss over all the successes prior to that?"

"What successes?"

"Your girlfriend passed out and left you alone, a blind kid, to deal with four bullies. You dispatched them easily *and* ultimately got the girl to safety." She paused for dramatic effect. "But you call that evening a failure."

"It's like baseball," I tried to explain. "A lot of things can happen in the course of nine innings, but all anyone at home watching on TV remembers is if the last guy at bat struck out to lose the game or hit a homer to win it."

"Hmm," she said. "So total victory or else all is a loss? What if the guy who hits the winning homer actually struck out four times earlier in the game, twice with runners in scoring position? Is his success at the end greater than his failures in the middle innings?"

"Yes," I answered, thinking I was confident.

"Let's stay with baseball, but reverse it," she offered. "A guy named Mike hits for the cycle in game seven of the World Series—a single, a double, a triple, and a homer." I wanted to be impressed with her baseball knowledge, but she was talking too fast for me to take the time. "But after nine innings the game is still tied. The opposing team takes the lead in inning thirteen, and Mike comes up in the bottom of that inning with a runner on base . . . and strikes out." She paused, letting me catch up. "Is Mike the goat of the series for striking out at a key time? Do his heroics the first nine innings now mean nothing?"

"Well, they don't mean nothing," I allowed. But that was all it took for her to pounce.

"So if his first four at bats were successful—and not only successful, but rare, in that he hit for the cycle—and those successes still count even though he struck out at the end . . ."

"I see where you're going," I cut her off. "And I guess I understand what you're saying from a logical standpoint. But emotionally . . . I still feel responsible. I still . . . I still feel . . . guilty." I burst into tears, sobbing into my hands as they covered my eyes.

One thing about therapy that's interesting is that you never know quite when a good cry is going to happen. And another good thing about therapy is that when sudden tears do occur, it's never treated as weird or annoying . . . because it's actually representative of growth.

My therapist handed me a box of tissues, which I received gladly.

I climbed in the passenger seat, shut the door, and put on my seat belt. Then I let out a large and long sigh.

My father had driven me to therapy today, in part because Emmaline was busy, and in part because I didn't want to abuse my girlfriend's teleportation abilities and treat her like my own personal taxi service.

Dad started up the car and backed out of the parking spot. The radio was playing Christmas music.

"Christmas music, already?" I asked. "Isn't it a little early for that?"

Dad pulled out of the parking lot onto the street. "Ask your brother," he finally replied. "He's the one who chose the station on the way to his yoga class."

Dad had enrolled Patrick in yoga classes two years ago in an attempt to help him meditate and slow things down. Patrick had taken to it—and had taken to a pretty girl in the class as well—and so Patrick was going on his third year of yoga.

"Figures," I muttered.

Patrick was more sentimental than I was. Actually, we were both sentimental, but he was more cliché about it . . . listening to Mom's favorite music, watching her favorite movies. I missed her just as much as he did, but at times he seemed to be trying to will her back into existence.

I just missed her. Life without her was reality, but life with her was a fine fantasy to escape into every now and then.

"I got a call from Emmaline's dad," he said, slicing through any and all wandering thoughts as he lowered the radio volume so we could talk.

"Oh man," I replied. "I can only imagine what he must have said."

"Well, he said he thought you were a bright young gentleman and he was glad his daughter was dating someone like you," Dad said.

"What!" I was shocked.

"It's true. He said all that. Just after he mentioned being frustrated at finding the two of you on her bed late at night."

"Dad," I began, "let me explain—"

"Let me guess," he interrupted. "You saved your and your girl's butts and then got teleported into her bedroom."

I shook my head in confusion. "How did you know that?"

"Educated guess," he said warmly. "I certainly didn't think you guys were . . . doing anything that . . ."

"Dad!"

Things were quiet for a bit while he drove. My therapist was local, so there were only a couple blocks left before we would be home.

"Do you know how proud I am of you?" he finally said.

"No," I answered honestly. "I screw up so much . . . I'm scared to know." I had never been so honest with my father. The pass-outs and panic attacks and nightmares had me on edge, and I found myself speaking more bluntly than ever.

"You think my being proud of you has anything to do with whether or not you make mistakes in life?" he asked with urgency.

"Doesn't it?" I seriously thought it did.

"Oh, son," he said, putting a hand on my shoulder. "I love you deeper than your life decisions, and I cherish your existence no matter your choices. You could screw up constantly and, while I would hope for better things for you, I would still love you."

And the tears welled up once again.

⚡

The best thing about being back home was reuniting with Sherpa. She loved Patrick, and I'm sure she was just fine while I was away, but she was bonded to me on a molecular level. Being back home meant she stood next to me in the kitchen whenever I was making dinner. It meant she slept on the bed with me at night. It meant she nuzzled me to check in on me any time my anxiety spiked or I was quiet for too long.

Tonight I was feeling a little overwhelmed with familial attention and decided to go for a walk with my dog.

Dad was in the shower and Patrick was playing a video game, so I left a note on the counter and took off into the night.

Mostly I just wanted to think, and that was tough to do with Patrick and Dad both making noise. Everyone needs some quiet time now and again; blind folks just need it a bit more frequently. Or maybe we just need it to be even quieter than most people require.

Sherpa and I walked around Freepoint in relative peace and quiet. Everyone was in for the night. We ended up at Donnie's tombstone, probably because I subconsciously led us there. And, once again, I spoke to my departed friend.

"Hey, Donnie. I miss you. I figure you are out there saving other worlds in the universe. Things were so much simpler a few years ago, but now it's all so complicated. It's harder than ever to know who I can trust. I could always trust you. You will always be my inspiration."

13

PERSUASION

"Persuasive speeches," Dr. Gates roared joyously. "A chance to challenge convention and to change minds!" She walked toward the back of the classroom—where she liked to sit during speech days. "Take a position, hold it firmly, and change my mind!" It was a challenge as much as it was a set of instructions.

Our first speeches had been impromptu, pulling a topic from a hat and trying to argue for it on the spot, just telling the class about ourselves and trying not to act too nervous in the process.

Now we'd graduated to speeches that meant something. We would do the persuasive speech, then we'd all give an informational speech, and finally we'd all finish with a motivational speech—which was kind of a hybrid of the informational and persuasive speeches.

"Mr. Sallinger," Dr. G called from the back, sending a chill down my spine, "you are *not* going first today."

Even as I breathed a sigh of relief, I also plotted ways to get revenge on my favorite professor. She enjoyed drama and practical jokes. She liked messing with our heads. I supposed in the long run it made us better public speakers, but in the moment it felt more like Wicked Witch–type stuff.

Instead of me, she called Nate first. As he was my only "friend" in this class, I decided to pay attention and feign enthusiasm for his arguments.

Turns out I didn't have to fake it. Nate's persuasive speech was about climate change, and I had long ago realized there was too much evidence for climate change to be ignored.

Nate was much better in his second speech than he had been in the first. It made sense, as the first speech had been impromptu so it lacked a cohesive argument. This one was scheduled, and Nate had plenty of time to research and prepare.

It showed. His arguments were emotional while also being supported by data. His speech's structure first laid out the problem and then suggested a few workable solutions.

I was sure he'd get an A. I subtly held out my hand for him to high-five as he walked back to his seat. It was a great way to start the class, giving all of us hope that our speeches might go even half as well as Nate's had.

Most of the rest of the students in the class had either ignored me or had been flat-out rude to me, so I didn't figure I owed them attention to their speeches. Instead I used the time to explore my own mind a bit.

While Patty Watson was talking about the positive impact of recycling . . . while Devin Harris was making good points about social networks and protecting our own data . . . even while Deborah Sterling railed against public education that had no biblical input . . . I was daydreaming.

I did a lot of daydreaming lately. As much as I could.

Mostly it looked like me and Emmaline growing old together and raising kids together and being happy and carefree. Usually there was a forest and sometimes a beach. Happy and carefree—that's how I knew the daydreams were lies.

I'd been a custodian for roughly seven years, and even I knew that it mostly led to heartache. I was only nineteen years old but already dealing with emotional and mental suffering directly related to custodian events. How was it going to get any better as I got older and did hero stuff more and more?

Suddenly I started replaying some of my life's most important motivational moments. Mom dropping me off at kindergarten after I got my ass kicked on the first day: "You belong here. Go nuts on anyone who doesn't agree."

I remembered my father's underwhelming pep talk before my first competitive chess match when I was ten years old. Dad said, "It's okay if you lose." Looking back, that almost seems like bad or lazy advice, setting me up for failure. But in the moment . . . it was exactly what I needed to hear. I'd been terrified of losing, and what losing would mean to my social status or overall value to the world. Having Dad say "it's okay if you lose" lifted a weight. I won my first two matches before taking a loss, and I'm sure it was because his clumsy attempt at fatherly advice ended up being the perfect salve for my self-doubt and apprehension.

I was just about to dive into a daydream about the far future, when I would be a father of my own kids, when I heard Dr. G's voice barking my name.

"Mr. Sallinger?" She had a tone that suggested she'd said my name seven times already, and maybe she had.

"Yes?"

"Now it actually *is* your turn, son," she stated.

I stood and tapped my cane as I walked to the front of the room; you never knew when someone's stray backpack or shoelace could cause a slip or a trip.

I'd practiced my speech for all of five minutes, and that had been last night. However, it was a topic I was knowledgeable and passionate about: statehood for Washington DC.

Everyone has that thing they were taught in middle school or high school that always stuck with them, for some reason or another. Everyone has memories that stick out from their education.

I remember vividly how angry I felt at learning in high school that residents of the nation's capital didn't have anyone in Congress to represent them. This was literally the reason America had been formed as a nation— to fight against taxation without representation. And here was the very most important city in our union, where we placed our government, and the citizens of that city had no representation.

I had no trouble spouting facts about this topic. I had no trouble getting worked up and emphatic about this topic.

But I didn't know if that would translate into a good speech or not.

I had note cards printed in braille that I barely used. I'd gotten a braille printer for Christmas my junior year of high school, and it could take any text from the web and turn it into braille on paper. I could even dictate to a microphone and the machine would spit out a braille version of what I had just said. It was amazing technology. I just got nervous enough in front of the class that I forgot the note cards and just started ranting.

I had made three solid points, and I knew the value of a three-point sermon, having been a regular at church much of my early years.

Point one: Every US citizen should be represented in Congress.

Point two: DC residents were not currently represented.

Point three: New legislation is needed, and we should all push for it to be passed.

I ended with a bit about my cousin, who lived in Tennessee and frequently complained about his vote not mattering, since he was a liberal living in a state full of conservatives. But DC citizens' votes mattered even less, because they had no vote, no voice, no representatives, and yet were still being taxed the same as Tennessee residents or residents of any of the other fifty states.

"Thank you, Phillip," Dr. G said pleasantly when I had finished.

As I walked back to my seat, I thought to myself, *Hey, you didn't pass out this time—that has to count for something.*

I left class in a hurry, because I felt embarrassed about my speech and I also wanted to get home as quickly as possible.

But Nate was just as motivated today. He ran after me and overtook me quickly. "Hey, man," he said enthusiastically, "your speech was awesome." I could tell he was faking, but it was still kind of charming to me.

"Yeah?"

"Totally. I thought you had good data to back up your arguments, and you made some good points that I had never thought about before."

"Alright, Nate," I said and smiled, "enough brownnosing. What do you want?"

He dropped all pretense instantly. "I want to go into the field with you," he practically shouted. "I want to be a journalist that focuses on custodial issues, and what better way to do that than to get practical experience in the field?"

"What are you asking me?" I stalled.

"Take me with you next time you go out superheroing," he said. "Let me tell the world what you're doing to help them. I can keep you anonymous if you want."

"You think my concern is about my identity?" I was laughing. "Dude, people know me. I'm out there. My concern is about your well-being! If I take you out with us, you are my responsibility, and thereby it's my fault if something happens to you."

"I'll sign a waiver," he countered.

"Screw your waiver," I retorted. "Waivers are made for lawyers to break with court arguments. Besides, I don't care about legality here, man, I care about your life! I care about my conscience. I care about right and wrong!"

"If you care about right and wrong, then you should want a neutral journalist observing things for the record," he replied. It was a knockout punch, mostly because he was right.

I sighed long and loud before finally admitting defeat.

"Okay," I said softly. "You can come."

"I think I did good," I said for the tenth time, trying to convince myself it was true.

Those of us who lived in Freepoint but went to college in Goodspeed met up every day at four o'clock on the campus quad near the fountain. Sometimes classes lasted longer or got out early, and everyone moved at different speeds, so we set this spot and time for a daily cutoff.

All classes ended at three thirty, so if one was late getting here by four it was probably their own doing. And they could always call Custodial Central for a ride. Custodial Central was kind of like a service hotline for custodians. If you needed a ride, or a particular tool or weapon . . . if you needed specific information found only in rare places . . . the Custodial Central guys had you covered.

Luc and Lacene lived in Goodspeed, so they always walked home. But Emmaline was tasked with taking home me, Patrick, Bentley, Penelope, Greta, Freddie, and some weird guy named Zerp, who never spoke and apparently didn't have any powers or ever engage in hero activities.

"I'm sure you did fine," Emmaline reassured me. I thought it was a good sign that, even though I was anxious about it, I actually cared about my school grade . . . and wasn't totally consumed with real-world hero stuff. My therapist would also later confirm this as a moment equal parts win and loss.

Greta showed up, cheery and ready to rock as always. That girl had energy to burn.

Next came Freddie, who was forgiven for moving slowly since his disability of asthma was known to trigger his superpower—gigantism—on reflex. Freddie moved slowly in order to make sure he could always go "full Freddie" when the situation demanded it.

Penelope was next, and I was surprised to hear her show up without Bentley. Emmaline and the others welcomed her verbally, and no one said anything about Bentley, so I knew he wasn't here.

"Where's Bentley?" I asked Penelope.

"I thought he was here already. I haven't talked to him since this morning."

We waited the assigned amount of time for Bentley to show, but he did not, and at the cutoff it was time for everyone else to get on with their evenings.

"I'm sorry, Penn," I said to Penelope before saying what everyone had concluded already. "It's time to go home. Bentley is on his own."

Emmaline moved into position in the center of the pack. "Everyone in," she called. A few seconds later—

Ooph!

We were back in Freepoint.

Most of the group were happy for the free teleportation ride back to their hometown and chose to hoof it home from here. Every now and then

Emm would need to teleport someone home to save time or even pain if they were injured.

Tonight everyone was off walking on their own, heading out from our Charles Field arrival point on foot, and Emmaline and I were left alone.

We walked in silence for a minute.

"You're worried about Nate?" she asked.

"I'm just tired of being responsible for people getting hurt or killed," I answered honestly. "Nate isn't a custodian, Emm. He has no powers. He's just a human with a journalism thirst."

"But if he wants to be on the front line, is it your fault?"

"I could keep him away from the front line if I wanted to," I responded.

"Yeah, but then that would make you a villain, stopping a journalist from doing his job. That's not you."

"I don't want to stop him . . . I just don't want to help him."

"You can't treat him differently than the rest of the team, P," she challenged. "His passion for journalism is just as strong as your passion for justice. If anything, he needs your help more than any custodians need it."

"I don't know how to help him, Emm," I said honestly. "I don't share his love of journalism, and I'm biased on what news about custodians constitutes the truth."

"Maybe he doesn't need you to share his love of journalism. Maybe he just needs you to care about him, like him, love him—the guy, the kid himself, not his opinions or objectives." She was an excellent orator.

"Can I just go to sleep tonight and maybe we take this topic up again tomorrow?" I asked as we walked up my sidewalk.

"Of course." Emmaline kissed me on the cheek. "I'll see you tomorrow, okay?" She squeezed my hand and walked away.

14

THE LEAD

Most of the gang was chowing down at Jack's as we celebrated the weekend and some time off from our studies.

Spirits were high, and it seemed like everyone was laughing and having a good time. That is, until Bentley arrived.

Bentley came in like a tornado—as much as a guy with leg braces can resemble a tornado—and turned everything on its ear by announcing that his computers had finally completed the image search and had found our electricity-hogging suspect!

"I have good news and bad news!" Bentley declared as he walked into the room. "I have found our mysterious power-outage baddie in half a dozen real-world surveillance cameras. But I still don't know where he's hiding." I heard him laying out photos on the table. "Here he is in Rome. Here he is in Los Angeles. Here he is in Rio. Here he is in London."

"Scoping things out for future energy heists?" I ventured.

"That's what I figure," Bentley agreed.

"What's he doing with all that energy?" It was rhetorical, and I wasn't able to hide the twinge of fear in my voice.

"Trouble is," Bentley continued, ignoring me, "these are all in the past. And because he's literally all over the globe, there's no way for me to know where his base of operations is. I need a live satellite feed coupled with facial recognition software and then . . . then we'll maybe be able to follow him."

"Well let's do that." It seemed obvious enough a decision to me.

"Can't," he shot me down.

"You don't have any live satellite feeds you can hack into?"

"I should have been more clear," he said. "I can hack into several databases that contain satellite and surveillance images and video—stored images and video. Those databases are on Earth, not up in the atmosphere. In order to get access to a live feed . . . we'd have to break into the Pentagon."

"Hmm," I pondered.

"Didn't you guys break into NASA a few years ago?" Freddie asked, wondering what the big deal was.

"We broke into a remote NASA storage facility," Bentley corrected. "It's not like we stole a rocket. Breaking into the Pentagon would be a lot more difficult."

"How come?" Greta asked between bites of pizza. "Can't you just teleport in, bada bing, bada boom?"

"We can teleport in easily enough, sure. But live video isn't a thing I can pick up, put in my pocket, and teleport back home with. I would need to monitor it. I would need to plug my own algorithm in, and that would certainly be detected. Aside from not damaging custodians' reputations any further, I just don't want to get arrested. And when you get arrested stealing from the Pentagon, you probably never get out."

I sighed long and loud.

"Is there a type of vision that sees energy?" Patrick asked.

"What?" I was mostly just being a big brother crapping on the kid's ideas here.

"What?" Bentley asked Patrick, much more seriously.

"There's night vision. There's infrared vision. There's all kinds of specialty vision goggles these days . . . I'm asking if any of them can see energy."

"Energy gives off heat, lots of it. Thermal imaging should do the trick. Why?"

"This guy is out there, somehow sucking an entire city's worth of electricity into some kind of small mobile container, and disappearing without a trace. But that much energy . . . maybe he leaves a trail." Pat was only guessing, but he'd never sounded smarter to me. "Maybe you can see that trail with the right lens?"

"That . . ." Bentley began, "actually makes sense." I heard him scribbling on a notepad for a few seconds. "But then I still have the problem of live video. I can't take stored images and apply a filter to it. I'd have to get to the source."

"The Pentagon," I added.

"No, the satellite."

No one said anything for a good thirty seconds. I heard some chewing and some straws being slurped on. Bentley was scribbling again. Someone blew their nose.

The satellite? I thought.

Suddenly Greta swallowed and decided to share a thought. "Why don't we just go to space?"

$$\text{\Large 4}$$

"I can't believe we're seriously gonna do this," I said, watching Bentley race around the lab gathering materials.

"It's fine," he said, not reassuringly. "There's been plenty of research on this subject."

"You want to send Emmaline into space without a space suit!"

"She doesn't need one," he continued. "The movies always get it wrong. Her head won't implode, she's not gonna freeze, her blood won't boil . . . as long as she's not out there too long."

"Well how long is too long?" I demanded to know.

"About fourteen seconds, give or take."

"Fourteen seconds!"

"This is so cool," Patrick said unhelpfully.

Greta was impressed as well. "This is, like, next-level blowing my mind."

"The biggest danger in space without a suit is ebullism. That's when the rapid change in pressure lowers the blood's boiling point below normal human body temperature."

"That sounds . . . horrifying," Penelope said.

"But that will take at least thirteen or fourteen seconds to happen," Bentley clarified.

"It was fourteen just a second ago, and now it's thirteen or fourteen. I'm not liking how unsure you are of all this," I complained.

"It's not like there's a lot of data to pull from. It's not like a lot of people have been in space without a suit before."

"I don't see why we should be the first," I said to no one in particular.

"There was a test subject at NASA in the sixties that was exposed to vacuum-like conditions, and he said he could feel the saliva on the end of his tongue boiling just before he passed out," Bentley said.

"Not really selling me here," I groaned.

"While I respect your opinion and your leadership, you're not the one I need to sell." Bentley dropped a small bomb there, letting me know that if Emmaline was okay with this plan, they would go through with it no matter what I thought.

I turned toward Emmaline. "Tell me you're not considering this."

"I'm considering it," she said truthfully and immediately.

"You . . . you forgot to say *not*," I pointed out, hoping against hope she'd misspoke.

"How much time could it take to teleport out, plant the camera, and teleport back? Like three or four seconds tops, right?"

Bentley didn't want to place a filter on the satellite's existing camera, because he was worried it would be detected. Besides, he'd added, the most expensive thing about the satellite was the housing of the camera and the cost in materials and fuel to get it up into space. The camera itself, while advanced, was something Bentley could approximate with cameras he could get his hands on here on Earth.

So he'd rigged up a super megapixel camera with a thermal vision filter. The entire contraption was about the size of a shoebox.

"So what? We use a magnet to attach it?" Emmaline asked, holding it in her hands and inspecting the device.

"Oh, no," Bentley corrected. "Too risky to use a magnet. Most satellites are made of lightweight metals like aluminum and titanium, both of which are extremely low on the magnetism scale. That, or they use metal alloys, like nickel-cadmium or aluminum-beryllium. But those are, again, too weak to be reliably magnetic. There are probably iron or steel components, sure, but without knowing which ones or where they are located . . ."

"So no magnets," Patrick summed up.

"No," Bentley confirmed. "We'll use glue."

"You want to send her into space with no space suit and a bottle of Elmer's!" The more I heard of this plan, the more I hated it.

"Actually, Phillip," he replied, "Elmer's would work perfectly, because dehydration is what makes that kind of glue get hard and bond. Water evaporation would occur even faster in space."

"I can't believe we're seriously gonna do this," I said for the second time in a few minutes.

The only other real challenge in this insane mission was figuring out how Emmaline would be able to teleport directly to the correct satellite.

Typically a teleporter needed some general idea of the location they wanted to go to, and then pictures, video, and even eyewitness accounts could provide specific enough details to get the teleporter close to the site.

But a government satellite orbiting the Earth? How was she supposed to zero in on such a location?

"I've teleported onto moving vehicles before," Emm said, defending her abilities.

"Yes, cars, trains, even airplanes—things you can see with your own eyes," I countered.

"Not to mention the speed difference," Luc added. "Those things up there are going a lot faster than a car, no?"

"Most satellites are traveling at speeds exceeding a few thousand miles per hour, yes," Bentley allowed.

"Why don't you sound concerned about that?" I wondered aloud. "That sounds like a problem. Isn't that a problem?"

"For some," Bentley allowed, "maybe. For us? We are able, after all," he said with a huge grin in his voice. "We can do this."

"Great. But how?" I urged.

"We just need to get her moving at the same speed."

"What!" I was about to lose my mind. I wasn't as smart as Bentley by a long shot, but I wasn't an idiot, and this sounded insane right out of the gate.

"Well, not the same speed, really, but the same pace relative to the planet's core."

"Zzzzzzzzz." Bentley had gone so far into science speak, Freddie had to fake snore to snap him out of it.

Everyone had a laugh.

"Okay, let's pretend this apple is Earth." I had no idea where he found an apple. I suppose he just had some sitting around in the lab in case he needed visual aids.

I heard the sound of the Earth apple being set on the table.

"And let's pretend . . ." His voice trailed off as he searched for another item for the demonstration. "Let's pretend this vinyl record is the satellite's orbit. And if we use this pencil as a guide, you can see that . . . a few centimeters on the Earth is actually a few inches out on the edge of the record. Does everyone see that?"

"Yes," they all replied.

"No," I said faintly. I instantly regretted my joke both because it was corny and because there weren't any other sightless people around to enjoy my blind humor.

"My point is, on Earth, Emmaline won't have to be going as many miles per hour as the satellite, she'll need to be going only as fast as it takes to keep pace with the satellite. I estimate it would be about . . . seven hundred miles per hour."

There were several gasps at such a large number.

"This is so rad," Luc said under his breath.

"Let me see if I have this straight," I began, my voice utterly dripping with skepticism. "You want to get Emmaline up to seven hundred miles per hour, somehow . . . directly under a satellite that is moving at a few thousand miles per hour up in space, so that she can teleport directly upward about one hundred fifty thousand feet and use Elmer's glue to affix a new camera to the front of a secret government satellite, all without a helmet or space suit or anything beyond her own Earth clothes?"

There was a pause, almost as though everyone was a few steps behind in processing.

Bentley finally responded with a simple, "Yes."

"How is she supposed to get going that fast?" Lacene finally spoke up. She had a tendency to lay back in group debates, mostly reading minds and trying not to use that information to keep the peace. Her powers were strong but willful, and she couldn't always control when she ultimately ended up spying on nearby thoughts.

"Patrick," Bentley declared.

"Patrick cannot run seven hundred miles per hour," I declared, factually.

"I bet I can," my little brother countered. He was hardwired to contradict me; I was just certain of it.

"I am not betting my girlfriend's life on it," I said, essentially shutting down the debate.

"Guys," Emmaline said, mostly to deaf ears.

"There's a track out in Arizona where they test rocket cars," Bentley said. "We could go out there."

"Rocket cars!" Greta exclaimed enthusiastically. "Cool!"

"I am not risking lives on a plan that contains so many 'ifs,'" I announced, trying to draw a line in the sand.

"Guys!" Emm yelled this time, and we heard her.

I turned in her direction.

"What if you just show me what it looks like and tell me when it's going to be directly overhead and by what distance? I do my teleporting instantaneously, so let's end this talk of getting up to speed or running seven hundred miles per hour. Just . . . give me the science of it and I'll trust it."

The bickering subsided, and Bentley pondered Emmaline's idea for a moment. It had been a long time since someone's common sense had cut through or changed Bentley's scientific precision planning. And yet, there was a confidence in her voice that sold the concept. It did sound easier, assuming her abilities really were instantaneous.

"Okay," Bentley adjusted, walking away for a moment to grab something. "This is what she looks like," he called while returning. I could hear him throwing photos on the table for Emm to see. "I know it looks small in this picture, but she's as long as a football field. You would want to aim for this nose portion here," he continued, the squeaky sound of a marker coming behind his words.

$$\lightning$$

We had to wait just over two hours for the satellite to pass directly overhead. We mostly filled that time with a movie. The crew chose the latest comic book crossover film, and while I'd heard it already I was happy to listen to it again. It was a crowd-pleaser for those with sight, and their reactions added new depth to my audio-only understanding of the film.

"It's time to get ready," Bentley called, just as the movie ended. "We have about five minutes."

"I can't believe we're seriously gonna do this," I said for the third time tonight.

"We need to find this guy," Emmaline said in response. "This is the only way we know to do that."

"I wish someone else could do it," I said truthfully.

"Ew," Patrick mocked. "Let's dispense with the sentimental crap, can we? We have a mission at hand here, and tears aren't going to help anyone!"

Emmaline got onto the platform Bentley had designated as the launching pad. She was wearing a pair of gloves and a ski mask, both of which would be worthless against the devastating attacks of space, along with her favorite blue hoodie sweatshirt.

"I'm ready," she declared.

I'm not, I thought.

She'll be fine, Lacene thought so only I could hear it. *She's the toughest chick I know.*

Thanks, Lace, I replied in thought.

Bentley was monitoring the screen showing the satellite's trajectory.

"Two minutes," he announced.

Everyone was already in place. Emm was on the stand. Penelope, Greta, and Echo were all positioned outside the rim to catch her in case Emmaline passed out before or after her trip.

"One minute," Bentley called, raising everyone's blood pressure a bit.

Sherpa was confused because I was anxious as hell but none of the environmental factors that typically caused my anxiety were present. So she knew I needed her help but wasn't sure what kind of assistance I needed most. And Emmaline's trip to space was so near, I didn't have time to stop and comfort my dog.

Everyone anxiously awaited the event. A few people said they were going to have their phones out to record things, but Bentley had already attached an HD action camera to Emmaline via a headband strap.

"Twenty seconds," Bentley called.

I nearly had a panic attack. I was so scared for my girlfriend's safety. While everything about the plan made scientific sense, it still scared the bejesus out of me.

"Here it comes, folks," Bentley said, monitoring the satellite's movement via his highly sensitive telescope. "Ten, nine, eight, seven . . ."

"Oh my god!" Patrick chirped.

I winked at Emmaline, even if I couldn't know for sure she was even looking at me. But if she was, I wanted her to feel a laugh or a smile right before the crucial moment.

"Three, two, one . . ." Bentley stopped counting.

Ooph!

I heard the distinct sound of Emmaline teleporting away. She was now in space, which was a deadly environment by definition.

Three seconds passed, and then—

Ooph!

Emmaline was back.

"Done," she declared.

A few seconds went by as everyone tried to process what had just occurred. Ultimately Emmaline had placed the camera with no problem and returned to Earth seconds later no worse for wear.

"Well, that was anticlimactic," Patrick said, speaking for all of us.

THE ABANDONED BASE

Nate Weller was more committed to his desire to be a custodial affairs journalist than I was to being a custodian. He woke every day at dawn, turned on three different regional police scanner radios, and started monitoring all the dark web messaging traffic he could handle—all just looking for the next great custodian news story.

He didn't even have anyone to publish his stories; he just put them on his own website.

He empathized with custodians without losing objectivity. He didn't want to glamorize them or sensationalize them. He just wanted to report the news. Specifically custodial news.

He heard a lot of chatter on the radio that he knew the Ables crew wouldn't be interested in or respond to. And because the Ables gang was his portal into that world, he wanted to stick with them if possible. He considered himself an embedded journalist tied to a special ops crew who hadn't yet caught a mission since he'd been stationed with us.

But it was Nate who heard about the European blackout and alerted us to the event before anyone else in the US was any the wiser.

The chatter got so loud on the back channels he monitored, Nate decided to wake me up. And while it was still too late for me or any of my friends to make a difference or stop this energy theft, I appreciated that he managed to follow his journalistic instincts while still slightly violating them to give me a heads-up on a possible battle or other custodial event.

Nate scored points with me that night, even if I didn't tell him so.

By the time we all woke up, London's own custodial heroes had stopped or stalled most of the general chaos that had followed the blackout. But we were ahead of all the American news cycles, and we had exact coordinates for our search fields.

And we finally had a reason to put our makeshift satellite camera to use.

"Let's see if the thermal camera caught anything out of the ordinary," Bentley said while firing up his laptop.

"There are a lot more trails than I expected to see," Bentley allowed.

We'd pulled down hours of footage from the camera Emmaline had attached to the satellite. Apparently there were streaks of light all over the place.

"I thought he was taking the electricity with him after he stole it," Bentley shared, "and storing it in a centralized location. But these lines suggest he's . . . he's *always* carrying the stolen electricity with him."

"How would that be possible?" I asked. "The sheer volume of energy he's stolen is far too large to be contained in any kind of machine or device that is portable. You told me that."

"That's my understanding of the science of it, yes, but this data doesn't support that. Everyone, look here." I heard the tip of his pointer hit the screen on the wall. "This is Boston. This is what a major city bustling with electricity looks like through the thermal filter. Now if, as we supposed, this guy was storing the stolen energy somewhere, there should be some place on this globe in these photos with three times as bright a footprint as Boston has. But there's not."

Freddie strolled into Bentley's lab and groaned something akin to a hello. We used a group text messaging app to communicate about Ables-related stuff—sudden meetings, practice changes, mission information, etc. So everyone had gotten the alert about London's blackout and to meet at the lab; Freddie just took longer to read it because he was the heaviest sleeper in the entire world. I once yelled his name right in his face and he didn't wake up. We were used to Freddie being a little late.

Everyone nodded or said hello back to Freddie and then turned back to the topic at hand.

"Is there any way for him to have hidden the heat signature of the energy? Like in a bunker or underground facility?" Patrick was proving lately to be a bit brighter than I'd bargained for. I preferred being the smarter of the two Sallinger kids.

"Not this much energy," Bentley said sadly. "Not with any materials I'm familiar with. I mean"—he walked over to the computer and tapped keys, apparently zooming out the camera angle—"you can see a faint circle in these images that is the core of the Earth. That's how powerful the thermal sensors are. So if we can see the planet's core, we'd see any underground store of energy for sure."

"So then where did it go?" Emmaline asked.

"I think he's taking it with him somehow." I could almost hear Bentley shrugging. "This line, I think this is him, zipping all over the world constantly. But the line at the center is twenty times brighter than the brightest heart of the city of Boston. Whatever this line is," he said and traced it a few times, following the path on the screen with his pointer, "man or machine . . . that's our missing electricity. I'd bet my life on it."

"Even though science says that's impossible?" I asked, mostly double-checking.

"Yeah," he admitted. "Science is nothing if not being willing to grow and change when confronted with challenging data. That's actually the definition of science."

"There are so many lines," Penelope said softly. Most of what Penelope said was said softly.

"How do we figure out which lines happened when?" It was Nate, who I'd brought with me since he'd been the one to initially alert me to the London event.

"Who the heck is this guy?" Freddie finally formed a complete sentence.

"This is Nate. He's a friend of mine from college," I replied.

"We have speech class together," Nate added cheerily.

"Oh," Freddie said, still not sure why there was a new guy.

I tried again. "He's the guy who alerted me to the blackout in London."

"Oh," Freddie replied, still sounding more annoyed than informed.

I gave up. "Well, his question's still valid. How do we figure out which line's which?"

"Way ahead of you," Bentley retorted. "These are just stills, but if you look at the live video—which I've sped up ten times speed for our purposes—you can see a few clear patterns." He pressed a button that probably started the video. "There are spots around the world that he visits with much higher frequency than any others."

I heard Bentley pull a wheeled stool toward him and then sit down on it to do some typing. "Some quick math shows us he's been in New York City three times in the last twenty-four hours. He was in London just twice in that time. And in Brazil a whopping four times—that might be his next target, actually. But he went to this remote spot in Western Canada twelve different times in the same twenty-four hours."

I heard murmurs of both confusion and understanding around the room.

Bentley just kept going without pausing for the stragglers. "Here's a position in Siberia where he's been ten times in the last twenty-four hours. And here's yet another spot he's visited a dozen times in the last day, smack in the middle of the Amazon rain forest."

"This guy's gotta be a teleporter," Patrick offered. "There's no other way for him to get around that far that often that quickly."

"Perhaps," Bentley allowed. "But I'm less concerned right now about his mode of travel than I am about that massive collection of energy and what it could be used for."

"So, the next move is . . . we go to these places where his visitation is peaked, one at a time, and see if we find any more clues, right?" I was ready to move.

These days I was thinking less and acting more, which I told myself was me being more authoritative and decisive, but which was probably me acting unpredictably as a way of rebelling against the lingering mental health issues

I was facing. Which is to say I was probably just acting out, and not acting very smart.

"Yeah," Bentley allowed. "I agree. I thought about splitting up, but we have only Emmaline for long-distance travel, so we might as well stick together."

"Nate," I said as I turned toward his last known location, "time for you to leave. Sorry."

"Yeah, no," he replied. "Totally get it. Thanks for letting me sit in on a planning session."

"Off the record," I barked back. "That was all off the record."

"I know, I know," Nate acknowledged.

Luc finally spoke up, but only to his sister. "Combien voulez-vous parier qu'ils choisissent le mauvais endroit pour commencer à chercher?"

"Comme si tu pouvais faire un meilleur travail," Lacene spat back.

"Peut-être que l'un de vous devrait choisir," Emmaline said, shocking the entire room into silence.

After several seconds, Luc finally exclaimed, "You speak French?"

"I speak a little. But I'm learning. So you two had better learn Portuguese if you want to keep having private-but-out-loud conversations in front of the rest of us," Emm declared.

"I didn't know you were learning French," I said, surprised.

"I study whenever you're not looking," she said, repurposing one of her favorite bits of blind humor.

Eventually Bentley got us all back on track. "Anyway, I think we should go to the Amazon first. It's naturally hotter and therefore a more logical place to try and hide energy or hide with energy."

"The Amazon?" Patrick was incredulous. "The actual Amazon? Like snakes and killer whatevers and . . . the real Amazon rain forest! Are we taking any weapons? Are we taking antivenom? Are we taking nets and bug spray?" Patrick could freak out about seemingly anything. I figured there was something in his speedster DNA that sometimes also sped up his paranoia.

I grabbed my little brother by the shoulders and tried to shake some sense into him. "We. Are. Superheroes. We can beat snakes and whatevers. Calm down."

I'd always thought of Patrick as just high speed. Earlier in life I'd called him a spaz. Later on I maybe thought he had ADHD. But he'd always been, for lack of a better word, excitable. Maybe it was just a by-product of his superpower. But every now and then he could have a meltdown in two seconds flat over something fairly innocuous. This was the first time I considered maybe Patrick just suffered from anxiety like I did and could benefit from the help of therapy or medication, as I had.

How have I never wondered that before?

"Are we good?" Bentley asked me.

I just nodded, assuming he was still looking at me. And he must have been because he then shouted, "Everyone in on three!"

Originally "everyone in on three" was a literal thing we shouted before teleporting, because there were only four or five of us tops and we could all fit in a single circle, hands inside on top of each other.

Over time, the phrase had morphed to simply mean "let's get ready to teleport." And our group these days was large. Me and Pat, then Emm, that was three. Bentley and Penelope, Freddie, Greta, Echo . . . five more, that made eight. Luc and Lacene brought us up to ten.

Ten was too many for a single all-hands-in circle. But teleporting worked as long as you were touching any part of the person's body, even if it was a head or shoulder instead of a hand. You could even touch the shoulder of someone else who was touching the teleporter and it would work.

Point being, Bentley's call meant that teleportation was imminent and we should all get in position.

We all fell in like normal, either laying a hand atop the hand pile in the center or laying a hand on the shoulder of someone who had a hand in the center.

"Here we go, folks," Bentley warned. "Three, two . . ."

I had my hand on Emmaline's shoulder, as usual. But between Bentley's two and one, I had the faint sensation of someone grabbing my untucked shirttail. "What the—"

"One," Bentley finished.

Ooph!

A dream surrounded me. At least it felt like a dream. Vivid sounds, abundant smells, a gentle rain from above. I could hear birds, monkeys, insects, and a dozen other animals. It was everything a blind guy could hope to experience in a rain forest.

As a person without sight, my world and my entire life was experienced via sounds and smells, and this place was teeming with things I'd never smelled and noises I'd never heard. The Amazon rain forest was, much to my surprise, utterly fascinating to me. It seemed like an alien planet.

It was, however, also entirely void of any kind of secret energy-hoarding base, or any kind of base at all, or even any kind of structure whatsoever—at least anywhere near the zap-in point, which had been calibrated based on the thermal imaging scans.

Meaning we'd struck out.

I took a single step, and my right foot landed in a pit of mud. "Well, great," I declared to no one in particular.

"People! This appears to be a swing and a miss," Bentley admitted after a few minutes of very gentle exploration.

"Where next? Siberia?" I asked, hopefully dripping with as much sarcasm as I was feeling.

"Canada's closer," Bentley responded, oblivious to my frustration and merely making good and logical sense.

"Close doesn't really matter," Emm said flatly. "We're teleporting."

I ignored her for the moment. "Okay, Canada," I agreed with an emphatic wave of my arms I was not even sure Bentley stuck around to see. "Anywhere but here, please."

"Everyone in on three," Bentley shouted while also trying to scrape mud off one of his leg braces.

Canada proved a lot colder than the Amazon rain forest, which I suppose I should have expected. But it was still a jarring change of environments that none of us had prepared for. We lost a good ten to twenty seconds just from people adjusting to the cold by sucking air rapidly and rubbing their hands together in an attempt to create heat.

In Western and Northwestern Canada, there were millions of uninhabited acres. Every now and then a reality show would venture in to feature some crazy survival challenge, but for the most part it was utter wilderness. Millions of acres of wilderness.

Which made it the perfect place to try and hide something—like an evil base.

In fact, within minutes of arriving, we found a nearby military base. The only problem was that it was abandoned. All the technology was WWII-era, and half the cave holding the base had been exposed to the open air after a recent avalanche.

"I thought this was going to be his Fortress of Solitude," Bentley said, referencing Superman's hideout in northern icy climates.

"Maybe it was," I added. "In the past."

"It made so much sense to me," Bentley continued. "Guy hoarding energy probably needs an air-conditioned place to hang out and cool off . . ."

"Looks abandoned," Freddie added. "It probably hasn't seen any kind of action in several decades, I would guess."

We were about to regroup and leave the base when our conversation unexpectedly gained a new voice.

"Leave," it said, echoing naturally, as though the speaker were in our midst. The voice was strangely layered and choral. The effect reminded me of those throat-singers I'd learned about and listened to in high school music class.

"Stop seeking me and you shall be spared."

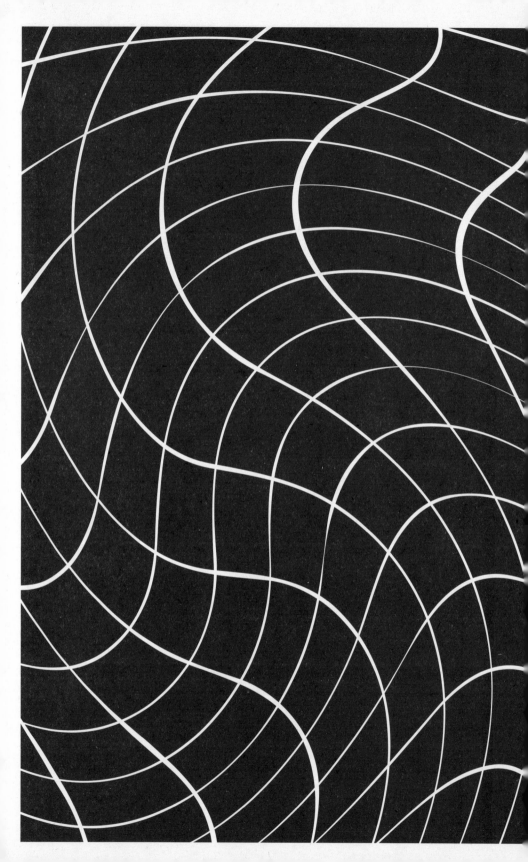

16

ADAM

"Who are you?" I asked defiantly.

"I am Adam. Why are you here?" His voice was deep, monotone, and full of reverb. Every time he spoke, it sounded like there were fifty of him, all speaking in unison.

After our encounter my friends would tell me that he was extremely tall, generally shaped like a human male, and appeared to be composed of energy that was alternately glowing blue and orange. My first mental image would be that genie from the animated movie I loved as a kid.

"You know why I'm here," I tossed out hopefully. It couldn't hurt to fish a little bit, could it?

"Why are you here?" the same voice asked again.

"I seek the one that is stealing electricity." I shrugged as I said it, because it was a total guess that I was speaking to the energy thief, even though it ultimately proved right.

"Why do you seek me out?" the choir-like voice echoed.

"You blacked out three huge cities," I replied flatly.

He didn't respond.

"Why are you stealing energy?" My voice was in full interrogation mode, even though I was honestly quite scared.

"The energy is needed by the master."

The room swelled briefly with an electronic shuffling noise that faded as quickly as it had started.

I didn't know how long this thing was going to talk to me, so I had to choose in the moment which follow-up question was more important: the one about the need for energy or the one about the sudden introduction of an ominous master. I opted to try for both in one fell swoop.

"Why does the master need so much energy?" I backed off the aggressive tone of voice, hoping to gain more information by appearing friendly.

"The machine needs much energy. The machine will fix the world. The master wants to fix the world." I couldn't see the colors changing in the being's form like my friends could, but I could hear them . . . flames lapping and morphing into crackling electrical current, and back again, like a metronome.

"What's wrong with the world?" I said indignantly.

"Everything," it responded.

"Says who?"

"The master."

"And who is the master, Adam?" I finally asked.

"The master is the fire. A burning is required." There was a dramatic pause, and then, "You will get no further information from me. Leave now."

"Leave?" I was incredulous. "We're just getting started here, bud."

"No. We are finished."

Bentley told me that Adam merely flicked a single finger in our direction.

We were all instantly transported back to the ER lobby of Freepoint Hospital.

For a few moments, everyone just gasped and groaned as they realized where they were and what had just happened. Massively strange events had occurred, and we'd also just been teleported by a new method that kind of tingled a bit, and we'd just endured another sixty-degree temperature swing in the last fifteen minutes, so our lungs were flustered.

"What?" Freddie yelled instinctively.

"What just happened?" I added, unhelpfully.

"Did he just zap us home?" Bentley sounded offended.

"What?" Freddie yelled again.

"Que diable?" Luc spat.

"Why don't we just go right back up there?" Freddie asked. "Clearly that guy wanted us to go away."

"Oh my god!" Penelope shrieked. "Emmaline!"

My heart began to race instantly.

"What?" I yelled. "What about Emmaline?"

"She's passed out, I think . . . unconscious," Penelope added.

"Oh no," Bentley replied. "Patrick is passed out too!"

"What?" Freddie yelled again.

"What?" I echoed.

Suddenly voices rang out from everywhere as hospital staff realized they had multiple emergency patients at once and started calling out orders and codes. An alarm blared.

I heard my friends' voices intermittently with the ringing in my ears.

"I know CPR."

"Wake up, Emmaline!"

"Back off and let the doctors take over!"

Some of the comments began to echo in my ears.

And that's about when I felt my world start to tilt. Another episode was underway, and even though I recognized it I was still powerless to stop it.

This is going to earn me another lecture from the doctors.

It's weird how time slows down when you're passing out from anxiety. You can hear so much that you can't actually impact or change. It's like double the punishment. Like my brain is telling me, "Yes, you're passing out, and here's all the terrible stuff you can't prevent while you're unconscious."

Sure enough, I awoke in my hospital room to a familiar situation: my father sitting on the chair in the corner and doctors Pulaski and Marvin standing at the foot of my bed. Granted, I didn't see them, but I heard them fine.

Once they realized I was awake, they pounced.

"Phillip, we'd like to admit you on a long-term basis here at the hospital," Pulaski began, speaking rapidly, as though hoping to prevent an interruption.

I could hear that Dad's breathing was aimed at the floor, which meant his head was likely in his hands, probably out of a feeling of helplessness regarding my mental health.

If he feels helpless about my mental health, how does he think I feel about it?

"We'd like you to consider a Nanite Rewrite."

I knew what it meant, but I was also still literally just waking up, and kind of resenting the hard sell on the invasive robot surgery into my brain so soon after I stopped sleeping.

"You"—I rubbed my eyes—"want to put nanite robots into my brain and give them control over it to help me be less depressed and anxious?"

"It's not quite that simple," Dr. Marvin tried to explain.

"Have you guys considered at all that my panic attacks and anxiety issues might be situationally inspired? In that we live in a world where kids like me and my friends put our lives on the line to save innocent people, and that is stressful and sometimes means we nearly get killed!"

"We'll talk again in the morning," Dr. Pulaski said, with a note of finality.

I heard the door open and close as they left, and then I sought out my father's counsel. "You can't seriously think this will help me, can you?"

He said nothing. I figured he was torn between the physicians' advice and the child's wishes and fears. But I didn't have a lot of time for his mental anguish, as I was facing some issues of my own.

"Do you think I need this therapy, Dad?" My voice shook a bit, quivering. This was the man who'd told me not long ago that he would love me no matter what. But sending me to nanite therapy felt like the opposite of love. It felt like prison. Torture. It felt like the rewriting of my brain, which it literally was.

But all I heard in response was a sudden snore. Dad had fallen asleep.

At first I was, of course, offended that my father had fallen asleep while my doctors were not only discussing my health but recommending a controversial and challenging line of treatment.

I was offended for a good hour—it's not like I had anywhere to go, and Dad's continued snoring only enraged me further for the first sixty minutes.

But eventually it dawned on me that Dad's job probably wasn't easy.

He'd lost his wife. Now he had a son in the hospital for the second time in a month, with a mental health issue traditional science struggled to treat or cure. That's all outside his own day-to-day life as one of the board members working closely with the US government to create laws around custodial activity.

The second and third hour I spent feeling guilty. Dad was exhausted— how could he not be—and I was a huge part of the reason. I wore him out and was now looking to him for help; it wasn't fair.

By hour four I'd made peace with things. Dad was asleep and that was that. I couldn't be mad about it after all I'd put him through.

But I didn't have to stay in this bed while he and the rest of the hospital slept. And since no one had given me any updates, I decided to go looking for whatever information I could find about Emmaline and Patrick, knowing only that they'd both been declared unconscious right before I blacked out myself.

⚡

I was blind, but I was also a regular at Freepoint Hospital. I knew the halls and stairwells very well, and I'd even "seen" much of the facility through Henry's eyes over the previous years.

I figured Emm was here, which seemed natural given we'd shown up in the ER together and there would be no reason to transfer either patient to Goodspeed or any other custodian hospital. And I figured she'd be in the intensive care unit, or the ICU.

Previous experience in this building told me the ICU was on the first floor, northeast corner. I was currently on the third floor, so I was going to have to navigate a stairwell or an elevator, both of which were a little tricky.

Where is the guard? I asked myself.

I tried straining my ears.

The hospital was low security, mostly because it was a superhero hospital located in a superhero city, and attacks of any nature were rare and not considered a serious threat. So there was one overnight security guard named Manny. He was a human-support worker who had a background in accounting and clerical work—in other words, he was a lousy security guard that I could easily avoid, if only I knew where he was.

My previous experiences in this facility had taught me that the guard loved the elevator and hated the stairs.

I couldn't hear any trace of him on the third floor, so I tapped with my cane until I reached the elevators and just waited.

Soon enough, I heard one of the elevator cars being called down to the first floor. It was time to move.

Thankfully, this building had placed the staircase and the elevator bays directly beside one another, so I had only a few paces to walk before starting my descent.

Throughout my life, I'd climbed up and down many sets of stairs, both while completely blind and for a few years with the assistance of Henry's telepathic vision. I knew how stairs worked. I wasn't worried about getting down the stairs.

I was worried about getting down the stairs to the second level, only to have the security guard exit the elevator on the second level and walk right past me.

I was halfway down the flight and on the landing by the time I heard the ding of the elevator's arrival on the second floor. Despite my confidence, I played it safe and stayed on the halfway-point landing to listen to the guard's movements.

The elevator doors opened.

I heard the guard grunt or cough. "I thought I pushed three," I heard him say. "Weird."

The doors closed again, and the elevator started up to the third and top floor.

I waited a moment to be sure the guard had stayed on the elevator, and then I continued down the staircase.

I paused to listen at the door to the second floor, mostly overdoing things since I knew the guard was up on three.

Satisfied, I managed the staircase down to the main floor and then used the wall handrail and my own memory to work my way to the ICU.

The Freepoint Hospital ICU was walled in on one side by glass. The intention of the design was to allow doctors headed into the ICU for surgery or patient visits to get a brief look at patient status and behavior before going into the session. It wasn't really intended to serve as a viewing gallery for patients' family members.

I turned down the glass-walled hallway intent on entering the ICU chamber directly, only to hear the voice of a friend.

"Hey, Phillip." It was Bentley. "You always have impressed me with your ability to get around on your own," he admitted.

"You do well enough yourself," I reminded him. "You beat me here, didn't you?"

"I only beat you here because they decided to commit you. Wait . . . that was tacky. *Admit* you . . . they admitted you, not committed you."

"Honestly," I declared, "same difference."

Bentley chuckled a bit.

"What do you see," I asked, being extremely literal.

Bentley understood. "Your brother and your girlfriend are still unconscious." He sounded a bit sad, but mostly like a guy who wasn't sure how to act the correct amount of sad.

"So energy guy Adam zaps us all back to Freepoint, but he leaves two unconscious?" I was asking myself as much as anyone else, but I said it aloud.

"Hmm," Greta said, out of nowhere.

"Holy crap, Greta!" I jumped three feet in the air. "You can't go sneaking up on people like that! You'll cause a heart attack."

"Oh." She paused. "Sorry. I didn't think about that. I knew you couldn't see me, but I thought your hearing was pretty good."

"It is," I assured her. "I was just distracted by, you know, being blind and my girlfriend and brother being hurt and stuff . . ." It was mostly a bluff, but it worked.

Greta continued. "I'm just saying . . . and it might not be important . . . but . . . he took out the only two Ables who could have quickly returned us to that base. That's interesting."

"So he didn't want us to return right away?" I parroted. "Why would we return after he just finger flicked us through time and space like a paper football?"

"The doctor earlier," Bentley started before pausing a few seconds, "he said he hadn't seen test results like this outside of lightning strike victims."

I was mostly operating on fumes and willing to embrace any positive explanation for recent events. "But most lightning strike victims wake up, right? Most of them are fine, right? Why haven't they woken up yet?"

"They will soon," Greta said confidently. "They will, I know it."

17

INPATIENT OUTPATIENT

The next day, when Dad did finally learn of the doctors' latest recommended treatment, he raised a ruckus and had me discharged immediately.

We had a nice moment in the car as he tried to apologize for falling asleep the previous night. I told him not to worry, and that I'd figured it out. That it was me who should be apologizing for being such a bringer of worry. Then he insisted he was the sorry one, and we went back and forth like a sitcom. Ultimately it ended in a hug.

It felt good. It felt good to again be reminded of Dad's love.

It reminded me of Bentley and his rocky relationship with his father. It made me wonder when Bentley had last had a moment such as this of his own.

"What am I gonna do, Dad?" I asked. "How am I going to stop these panic attacks?"

"I don't know, son," he said. "But we will figure it out." He paused a bit while he drove. "Didn't your therapist recommend something you said sounded too much like Star Trek?"

"Yeah. E something." I paused, trying to remember. "EMDR, I think. Lights and bad memories or some such. Sounded like a bad sci-fi movie."

"Hmm."

I hated when Dad said "hmm."

"Lights sound a lot better than nanites," he said, leading me.

"Yeah," I admitted.

"Can't hurt to try it, can it?"

"I guess not."

"Let's start there, and then we'll take the rest of it one day at a time."

"Yeah, alright."

"And I want you to start taking the dog with you more places."

"Sherpa?"

"No, the other dog."

We did not have another dog, but sarcasm was a family trait.

"Why?"

"Part of the whole point of that dog is to help you with the anxiety and help you avoid having panic attacks. But you don't take her everywhere. You don't take her to all your classes. You don't take her on all your missions. You leave her with me sometimes, when you go on dates or whatever. She needs to be by your side at all times, period." Your last two blackouts happened while Sherpa wasn't around."

I'd come to love the dog like a friend. "But what if something happens to her?"

"But what if something happens to you?" he retorted.

We drove a bit more. I knew the route so well by feel and sound and timing I could probably have actually driven the car home from the hospital myself. It was barely a few miles.

"I have to drop you off and then go into work for a bit," he said. We turned into the driveway. "I'll call you as soon as I hear something about Patrick or Emmaline."

"Okay."

"Love you, kid."

"Love you too."

I got out and walked to the front door and went inside to an extremely excited-to-see-me Sherpa as Dad backed out and drove off.

After giving the dog some much-deserved attention, I let her into the backyard and made a beeline for the phone, punching in a relatively new phone number I'd stored in my brain.

"Hello?" Nate answered.

"Did you have a good time?"

"What do you . . . what do you mean?" He was being cautious, not sure what I did and didn't know.

"Are you going to make me spell it out for you, or do you just want to come clean?"

He stammered a bit but struggled to form a reply.

"Alright," I finally said. "You were there last night. You jumped with us to Canada and you got zapped to the hospital with the rest of us as well. I heard you say you knew CPR right before I passed out."

He heaved a massive sigh. "Yeah," he said. "I grabbed your shirt right before the jump. I was terrified the entire time, and I promise I'll never do that again."

"That's a huge violation of trust, man." I sounded disappointed, because I was. "It's bad enough you endangered yourself needlessly, and endangered everyone else as well. It's even worse that you did it in secret. I'm responsible for lives out there, and I at least deserve to know how many I'm trying to protect."

"You're right," Nate said meekly. "You're right about everything. I won't ever lie or be sneaky like that with you again. It made me sick to my stomach, as a journalist."

I had to admit he sounded legitimately remorseful.

"Alright," I finally said. "I'll see you in class."

"Okay, see you in class."

I went to the back door and called for Sherpa to come back inside, and then I turned on the TV and lay down on the couch to take what I thought was a much-deserved nap.

"Come here, girl," I called, and Sherpa jumped up and lay beside me, resting her head on my chest.

On the TV, an old movie was playing. It sounded like some kind of cops and gangsters film noir kind of thing. There were a lot of screeching tires and bullets being shot. You know, perfect kind of thing to fall asleep to.

I was out in seconds.

I dreamed again that I was on a large raft.

In the water appeared the souls of my departed friends and family members. Mom. Henry. James. They floated alongside the raft and called out, telling me to join them in the water.

I looked up and realized I was passing the same crooked oak tree I'd noticed a few moments earlier. This river was a circle.

I felt something on my ankle and turned to see Henry's ethereal hand. Before I knew it, he'd pulled me into the water.

I felt heavy and began to sink, my hands flailing about trying to grab hold of the edge of the raft. My right hand found a grip, and I managed to pull my head back above the water. A figure appeared on the far end of the raft and slowly walked toward me.

It was Donnie!

I shouted in joy at seeing my friend again. He knelt at the end of the raft and smiled.

"I've messed up so bad so many times, Donnie," I confessed. "I broke things . . . people."

Donnie put a single finger up to his mouth to quiet me, and then he said, "Don't worry, Phillip. Donnie fix." Next his giant right hand reached toward my face, and he pushed me under the water, holding me there until I was nearly drowned.

That's when I woke up.

The phone rang immediately, and I thought for a second the ringing might have been what woke me up. Regardless, I reached out my hand and pulled the receiver across the room to me. "Hello?"

"I've called you three times!" It was Freddie. "They're awake! Get over here!" He then hung up abruptly.

Just then I heard tires squealing outside as Dad pulled into the driveway. I heard him running up the walk before he opened the door and simply said, "Let's go!"

Emmaline and Patrick were in different rooms, each with their families with them. Outside in the waiting area sat Luc, Lacene, Greta, Echo, Penelope, Freddie, and even Nate. Bentley wasn't there, but it would be the next day before I realized or remembered that. Anyway, he could have been up to anything, and it was still impressive to see how many had turned up once the news broke that their friends were awake. It was after nine o'clock at night.

Both unconscious members of my Ables squad had awoken at the exact same time, and they had since received a barrage of tests. They were in perfect health, though the hospital was going to keep them overnight just for observation.

Sherpa was such a good dog that she even gave Patrick a little extra attention, licking his hand and nuzzling up to the bed.

Dad seemed relieved. Twenty-four hours ago both his kids had been in this hospital as medical question marks, and now they were both awake and well.

I didn't get a chance to visit with Emmaline privately, but I was allowed into her room while her family was there to give her a quick hug and say hello. I hoped she could hear the relief in my voice, even though the environment wasn't conducive to me just blurting out "I care about you!"

"They're going to let me out of here tomorrow, so we can talk more then," she said, squeezing my hand with hers.

"Alright. Really glad you're okay."

I said my goodbyes to her parents and made my way down to the waiting room, where everyone was excited to get more news.

Everyone seemed genuinely happy and relieved. There were a bunch of hugs. Eventually everyone made their way to their respective homes to go to bed.

Even after all that, Dad still had to go back in to work. I had a feeling one day I was going to hear the stories of what he was working on during this time in his life, but it had to be stressful, if only due to the sheer number of hours he was putting in.

He offered me a ride home, but I'd taken a nice nap and had some energy, so I decided to walk home with Sherpa.

I loved taking walks with her. When Sherpa was with me, I didn't have to use my cane. She did all the navigational work.

There was a smell in the air tonight that I recognized as the scent of autumn. Temperatures would be dropping in the coming days, and the leaves would start to fall.

"What do you think, Sherps?"

I liked talking to the dog as a way of working through things sometimes.

"What is this Adam guy's deal? Who do you think his master is? What kind of machine could fix the world? What's wrong with the world?" I paused, considering that statement, and then followed it up with, "What's not wrong with the world?"

Sherpa turned us left at the corner of Jefferson Street. She was a bit like a GPS for your car, in that sometimes the route chosen didn't seem to be chosen for any particular reason. Sometimes she would lead me straight at that corner and not turn left until Baker Street. Other times she would have made the turn a block earlier on Wilmington. Tonight we turned left on Jefferson. And I would never get to understand why. She either had her reasons or she didn't. But I always followed where she led me.

"What kind of machine could fix all the many problems in the world?"

A dog inside a house we were passing started barking at us. Sherpa was great about not getting into shouting matches with other dogs.

"Wait. Why am I assuming this master is sane? He's orchestrating the theft of massive amounts of electricity—why would his assessment of the problems in the world be based on any common moral or logical understanding?"

My friends and I had faced many kinds of villains. Some were logical and at least had a reason one could make sense of. Others were just insane. I hated the insane villains, like my own grandfather—my first real villain. Nothing about an insane villain was predictable.

"How do we stop a man we know nothing about and who we cannot find? Is this Adam guy even a man? Is he a machine?"

We turned again, this time onto our own street, still a few blocks from home.

"Why did he zap Emmaline and Patrick and no one else? Was it really because they were the only ones with powers that could have taken us back to the abandoned base rapidly? Why did he think we would do that if he was capable of just flicking us away like he did?"

We paused at Allen Avenue, because Sherpa heard a car approaching. After it passed, we crossed the street and continued home.

"Maybe he didn't think we wanted to come right back but just needed to make sure we didn't." Sometimes my brain does this thing where it just kind of clicks and a realization is born. "Why didn't he want us to come back? What was he trying to keep us from seeing?"

I rolled that around in my mind for a moment or two as we walked, just one block from home.

"Hmm," I said. Saying "hmm" when you think you are about to make a good point is just one of many traits I'd frustratingly picked up from my father.

We turned up the driveway and walked to the front door.

"We have to go back there, Sherpa. We have to go back."

18

LOS ANGELES

"I like Los Angeles!" Freddie glowed. It was the first time in LA for nearly half the crew.

"Try riding in a car here sometime," I sniped. "That'll clear you right up of that notion."

"Ha," Bentley laughed in agreement. He'd gotten everyone all riled up this morning with a group message about an algorithm he'd created to predict the next city Adam would try to rid of its electricity.

I'd tried bringing up my realization from the walk home with Sherpa— that maybe we should check out the base in Canada again—and he shut me down pretty quickly. "That was a dead end" is actually what he'd said, which was patently absurd. But I thought maybe he was just so excited about his new bit of code-writing he didn't have time for anything else.

He'd also surprised Luc with a new gadget. It was essentially a metal headband composed of a unique blend of minerals and metals in a way Bentley said would amplify the range of Luc's EMP powers by at least 30 percent.

Bentley seemed to be inventing a lot more lately, and I thought it was a good sign. His animosity levels were down considerably, too, both in regard to his father and to me. For nearly two years following Henry's death, Bentley had pushed me away and kept me at a distance, at times treating me coldly. But these days it was like we were the old friends we'd been way back that first year when we'd met. He was even laughing at my jokes again.

It was midmorning on a Saturday, and we were standing in front of Grauman's Chinese Theatre in Hollywood.

"This is the center?" Lacene asked. "The most tourist trap cliché place in all of LA to visit?"

"Hey, I didn't pick it, the algorithm did," Bentley defended himself.

"But you wrote the algorithm," Lacene countered.

"I write code, but I don't force solutions," he explained. "The math does the work, and math is constant. You can trust math."

"I for one," Greta chimed in, "have never trusted any subject I can't earn better than a C+ in. So that includes math, grammar, and art."

"You don't trust art?" Patrick asked.

"Yeah," she replied. "That's right."

Bentley just kept going, like he did frequently when he was giving out knowledge and the conversation derailed. "This is the center. Not the geographical center. Not the electrical center. But the geographical-electrical center."

"That doesn't make sense," I replied.

"That doesn't even sound like English," Emmaline agreed.

"It basically means that this is where I would stand if I wanted to pull the electricity of all of LA's greater area into myself in the fastest and most efficient way."

"Alright, so this is the area you think Adam might stand in, if and when he comes for the power in LA?" I was just trying to keep up, mostly.

"A four-block radius, but yes."

"But . . ." I was still confused. "Are we just supposed to wait here, like, days and days until he maybe shows up? Even if your algorithm is right about this being the next city he hits, how do you know when?"

"Glad you asked," he said, grinning.

I immediately knew I was going to regret the question.

"I looked at the three previous attacks, and they've been occurring at a rate that is interesting. The second attack occurred exactly thirteen days after the first. The third was exactly eleven days after the second. Those are both prime numbers."

"I think I have a teleportation hangover," I sighed. "Can someone translate that?"

"No," Freddie said, sounding frustrated.

Then Bentley himself responded by just continuing. "There's a known relationship between electricity and mathematics. It's not out of the question this guy might be following some kind of pattern or set of rules. Maybe rules that include prime numbers. And the next prime number is seven, and today is exactly seven days since the London blackout."

He had a way of sounding so smart that you most often just got beaten into submission and agreed with him even if you were more lost than anything else.

After processing his argument and realizing he had a good point, I still had questions. "But still . . . we're here in the morning. What if he doesn't strike until tonight? We're just supposed to walk around here for eight hours?"

"I figured we'd take shifts," he said. Bentley seemed to have an answer for each and every question I was throwing at him, and it was growing annoying. "Half can go in and see a movie, the rest walk the area and patrol, and then we switch after a couple hours. Everyone keeps their radio earpieces in." I felt like he shrugged afterward. I couldn't prove it and I definitely didn't see it, but I felt a shrug in his voice.

Easy enough, I figured. "There's ten of us, five and five. We should probably split Patrick and Emmaline up, just so both groups have a hasty mode of transportation. Does anyone feel like taking the first patrol shift?"

"I would actually love to," Bentley said. "Pen, you wanna join me?"

"Of course," Penelope agreed.

I heard a whooshing sound I knew all too well. It meant two things: that Patrick had just raced off somewhere and that another whooshing sound for his return was imminent.

And then I heard it.

"I wanna see the new John Jupiter movie," Patrick said, "and that doesn't have a showing for another three hours, so I'll take first shift as well."

"Ugh," Emmaline said. "How do you watch that trash, Patty?" John Jupiter was a former wrestler who'd discovered a much more lucrative career in film, due mostly to his charming personality and uniquely bulbous muscles. Most of his films were big, loud, dumb, and poorly written. But people loved him, so his films made a lot of money. As long as he showed off his muscles and said a few cute one-liners, the audiences ate it up, including my brother.

"It's only trash if you don't find it entertaining," he retorted.

"That . . . no, that was a terrible comeback," I teased.

"That was a terrible sentence, period," Emm added.

"Whatever, I'm first shift. That means you two fools are second shift, so go watch your not-entertaining movie about some former British queen being bossed around by men or whatever."

He whooshed off again, probably only a block or two away, mostly to make a "storming out" kind of statement.

"So that's three first shifters. Luc and Lacene, do you guys want to be on the same team or different teams?"

"Same," Lacene said.

Simultaneously, Luc said, "Different."

I chuckled. "Twins," I said, shaking my head.

"Same," Luc finally said, agreeing with his sister. "We'll go first shift."

"Okay," Bentley summed up, "that means Greta, Echo, Freddie—you're all second shift. Go with Phillip and Emmaline and enjoy your movie."

The famous theater, now technically called the TCL Chinese Theatre, had one huge main auditorium that sat nearly a thousand patrons at once. But there were several smaller auditoriums playing other movies—six in fact. Four were 117 seaters, one held 237 seats, and the sixth and final came in at a rather large 458 seats.

All told, there were seven movies to choose from. Patrick's John Jupiter movie, titled *Bad Intentions*, had a stranglehold on the main auditorium, but the next showtime wasn't for a few hours, because it was a long film and had already started when we'd arrived.

Following my father's strongly worded advice, I had brought Sherpa along on this mission, and was happy to hear that the theater was friendly to service animals. We didn't even have to buy an extra ticket for her. Once, an amusement park had charged me an extra admission for Sherpa to come with me, can you believe that?

Emmaline had standing permission to always choose the movie, since I could typically experience only half of the film—the audio portion.

Still, she read me the alternative choices, because she was fair-minded and wanted my input.

"Here we go. Based on shows starting soon, we have five choices. There's an animated family film about a misunderstood weasel titled *The Vermin*."

"Ugh," I said out loud.

"There's a sports movie about a group of underdog volleyball players called *Bump, Set, Spike*."

"Eww," I said, a bit too honestly.

"There's a courtroom drama/romance where the prosecutor falls for the judge, starring that Italian guy and the hot cougar from that sitcom you hate. It's called *May I Approach the Bench?*"

"Oh man," I said with enthusiasm. "That's the leader in the clubhouse, I guess."

Emm continued. "We have a heist film about a crew of garbage men robbing the Metropolitan Museum of Art for millions while simply doing their job."

"New leader in the clubhouse," I declared. "That sounds amazing."

"Agreed," Emm allowed before finishing her descriptions. "Finally I have an indie film about an astronaut that returns to Earth smarter than anyone ever recorded."

"Is there an alien angle to the story?"

"I don't think so. The poster says the movie is introspective."

"Yikes," I said in disgust.

"So we're choosing the garbage man heist, I take it?" Emm asked, mostly just to make sure.

"I have to find out how that one goes—100 percent yes!" I added.

I didn't ask for headphones this time. I had mostly resolved myself to the idea that movies were going to be an audio-only media format for me but that I could still find enjoyment attending them with sighted people like Patrick or Emmaline.

⚡

Our movie came and went with a few laughs and a few interesting plot points, but no radio contact from the first watch Ables out on the streets.

Emmaline and I exited smiling, laughing about our favorite parts of the movie we'd just experienced and mocking the others' choices. Sherpa seemed happy enough, though she was still wearing her work vest so she was on alert.

We paused when we reached the main sidewalk, which was heavy with foot traffic as it was part of the Walk of Fame, where entertainers' names were enshrined inside star sculptures placed inside the cement walkway.

I reached up and pressed the "send" button on my radio earpiece. "Phillip and Emmaline, second watch, reporting for duty."

"Great," I heard Bentley say through my radio earpiece. "All first watch personnel report to the Grauman's Chinese Theatre entrance ASAP."

"Hey," came Greta's voice, "we're here too." She wasn't using the radio; she was just speaking to Emm and I in person. Echo was with her.

"What movie did you guys see?" Emmaline asked them.

"*The Vermin*," Greta said, giggling a bit. "No points for originality, but we enjoyed the pratfalls, and whoever did the voice of the weasel was pretty funny."

There was a mild silence, and I thought I heard slight movement nearby. Greta confirmed it. "Echo just signed that she laughed more at this movie than she did at the last Toby Norman film."

"Toby Norman?" I said in mock distress. "Oh, Echo, you have so much to learn about movies," I said like a know-it-all, even though I'd seen only 10 percent of the movies I'd been in attendance for and had merely listened to the other 90 percent. I thought I had more credibility in this discussion than I ultimately did.

"Toby Norman?" Lacene said in shock. "He made an entire movie where the main joke is that French people are stupid. Ne commence même pas avec moi à propos de ce connard."

Emm leaned in and whispered a summary of the translation. "She said some derogatory things about Mr. Norman."

"Okay," I declared. "Let's get back on track here, people. Second watch is taking over. We need to split up and cover a four-block radius. First watch is free to goof off and go watch a movie, even the John Jupiter one."

"How do you want to split things up?" Freddie asked. He wasn't using the radio; he was standing right next to me. Whichever movie he'd chosen to see had been the last to get out, but we were all accounted for now.

"Emm and I will take Hollywood Boulevard. We'll go east and west, two blocks in both directions. Freddie, you take the north and go at least two blocks up for every street. Greta, Echo . . . you guys take the south, and make sure you go both east and west once you go south."

My own words started to sound like mush to me. I was tired and out of my element but still responsible for all these lives.

"Did that make sense?" I called after them.

"Yeah."

"Yep."

If Adam showed up here on my watch and we missed him, I would never hear the end of it.

Emm and I walked arm in arm down Hollywood Boulevard moving east to west. We then crossed the street southbound and walked back the other way for four blocks. Sherpa learned the route immediately and started taking the lead on just the second time around.

We were acting like a regular LA couple out for a stroll, even though our real-life dating had been stuck in second gear for a couple of years. We were better at acting like a couple than we were at actually trying to be one. The irony wasn't lost on me.

And yet, despite the lack of much forward progress, things were completely comfortable. We were becoming good friends at the same pace, or maybe even a little faster, than we were falling into a romantic type of relationship, even though that felt like an implied eventual future.

We did a few laps, making a full square every time, before finally finding a lead.

"In front of us," Emm whispered, "fifty yards. There's a guy in a Chewbacca costume."

"It's part of the tourist attraction for the Walk of Fame," I explained. "People dress up like movie characters and try to get tourists to pay money to pose with them for a photo."

"No, I know all that," Emmaline rebutted. "But this guy I'm talking about in the Chewbacca costume is actually Chewbacca-like height. Easily eight feet tall." She paused briefly before finishing her thought. "I mean, that Adam guy was super tall."

"Do you have a pair of team glasses?" I asked as we kept our same pace, not wanting to panic.

"Yes," she responded.

"There's a thermal vision setting. Put them on and switch to thermal. If it's him, you'll know it right away."

I heard her fish through her backpack a few seconds, and then she stood back up. "Let's see what you're made of." She paused a beat and then sighed.

It was the kind of sigh that could have gone either way, so I had to get proactive. "So is Chewy insanely hot inside that suit?"

"He lit up like a Christmas tree," she said, giggling at the prospect of action.

"Let's put the harness Bentley created on now. I think things are about to get violent."

"You bet," Emm replied.

The harness locked her arms in with both of mine, but it also included a waist bracket that would ensure we remained connected even if I left the ground and took flight.

It wasn't lost on me that this harness Bentley built also allowed Emmaline and I moments of extreme closeness and nonromantic physical intimacy, which could be problematic or maybe just weird.

"Hey, Chewbacca!" I screamed, loud enough to get the attention of pretty much everyone on this block.

Emm said later that the over-tall Chewbacca suit guy stopped in his tracks right then.

"Yeah, you," I continued taunting, not knowing in the moment that he'd already stopped. "Turn and face the music," I yelled. "Turn and drop the disguise."

"He's already turned," Emm whispered.

"I told you to stop pursuing me," came a voice in front of me. It was Adam, the same electro-choral pulsing quality in his speech. There wasn't any doubt anymore. Bentley's algorithm had been right, and we'd caught the energy thief in the act of another heist.

I pressed a button on the radio earpiece. "Target acquired on Hollywood Boulevard, just outside the theater. Act now, move quickly." Then, to the dog, "Sherpa, stay!"

19

BATTLE

"This guy flicked us all across the globe while also making me unconscious last time," Emmaline said as we braced for battle. "What are we even thinking here?"

"Well . . ." I said, breathing fast.

"You are too late," Adam said, and then he let loose a scream.

"He's started the blackout," Emmaline said, alarmed.

"It's taken only a few seconds to occur in the previous cities. We have to try and stop him or slow him down!" I was shouting, trying to overcome the raw electrical noise. As electricity passed by us on its way to Adam's position, I felt static shocks on my fingers, arms, and even on my head.

"How about a force field around him?" Emm suggested, implying we try to block some of the electricity he was stealing from getting to him.

"Good. Give me some specs and point me in the right direction."

"Let's say ten feet tall, eight feet wide, and eight feet deep. Full power deflective pulse. Are you ready?"

Boy, was I ever. "Let's do this."

Emmaline swung her arms to directly aim them at Adam's position, and the harness brought my arms along for the ride. "Now!" she bellowed.

One of the more recent telekinetic tricks I'd learned was to use my abilities to create shields or force fields—walls essentially made of air and my push/pulse ability. It took too much concentration and energy to make it a long-term solution, but in plenty of battlefield situations, it could stand in temporarily to buy time until we found a better, longer-lasting solution.

With all my might I pushed against Adam's location, guided directionally by Emmaline's movements, bringing an invisible box down over Adam's head.

"I think it's working," I said between grunts.

"It is!" she agreed.

The flow of electricity to Adam hadn't stopped, but it had slowed significantly.

I heard the whoosh of Patrick's arrival.

My radio call had caused everyone who received it to panic and head for the location I'd blurted out, which meant that Patrick had no clue where anyone else was because they were all running on their own. So he just came to our spot and asked how he could help.

"Do you remember that time you were doing circles in Charles Field, after the drought summer, and you accidently created a dust storm?"

Patrick recalled the memory and then began to giggle. "Yes."

"Gotta be an empty dirt-filled lot around here somewhere, no?"

"There's a canyon right over there," Emm said. She paused while showing Patrick the location. "Can't be more than five hundred yards."

"I'm on it," he said before whooshing away.

"I don't think we can hold this back for long," I admitted.

"Yeah," Emm agreed.

Suddenly Freddie arrived, already in giant mode and ready to act. "What's going on? Status!"

"We've got him pinned inside a box of Phillip's push powers, blocking him from sucking in new electricity," Emmaline shouted. "But it's temporary. He's too strong."

Just then Adam nearly got loose, and I had to redouble my efforts and concentration.

"You want me to go punch him hard?" Freddie asked.

"No!" I blurted out. "Water!"

Emmaline interpreted my one-word message correctly, somehow, and said to Freddie, "Water and electricity don't mix. Go find a water tower or water tank. When we can't hold him anymore, we'll have you smack him with it."

"Done," Freddie said, stomping away, creating cracks in the street as he ran.

"We need Luc," I said. Luc's EMP ability was one possible way to end this standoff. At the very least it would knock out all the electricity in a nearby radius—a bigger radius than ever before with Bentley's new invention. Beyond that, it might even paralyze or otherwise immobilize Adam, who seemed to be made up mostly of electricity.

Greta and Echo showed up next. "What can we do? Hey, where is everyone else?"

"Freddie's looking for water, and Patrick is looking for dirt," Emmaline replied.

Our bodies collectively leaped off the sidewalk a couple inches as Adam grew closer to breaking our hold on him. All around us, electricity hung and hummed in the air, still being pulled to his position—such was his power—but mostly blocked by our temporary force field from reaching its destination.

"I can blind everyone with intense light," Greta reminded us. "And she can touch things and learn information about the item's past and stuff." She paused. "We're pretty useless here, right?"

"I don't know," I replied honestly. "Do you think you can go bright enough to blind an eight-foot giant that seems to literally eat electricity for lunch?"

"No idea," she said, and this time I definitely heard a shrug. "But back in DC when I first showed off my powers, I only used about 10 percent."

She'd saved our butts in DC, and I remembered people talking like it was the brightest light ever conceived. But only 10 percent?

"Alright, that sounds good, Greta," I agreed. "If he escapes my telekinetic prison, which he will, you try and blind his ass." I turned to where I thought Echo was standing. "Echo," I began. I knew she could read lips, and hoped she was looking at me. "Your power is super helpful, but right now I'm not sure it helps us win this battle and I'm more concerned about your safety. Stick close to me and Emmaline for now, and stay a few yards behind our position relative to Adam, okay?"

Adam continued wriggling fiercely, spouting off guttural roars, threatening to escape our trap at any second.

"Sorry we're late," I heard Bentley shout as he and Penelope arrived. "I don't move very quickly, you know," he explained.

I skipped the pleasantries. "Penelope, I need rain and a dense fog. The rain might mess with his electricity heist or his physical makeup, and the fog will let some of us get closer undetected."

"You got it, Phillip," she replied.

"What about me?" Bentley asked.

"You and your algorithm got us into this mess," I snapped. "Use that big brain of yours to figure out a way to capture this guy once we stop him from stealing more power—if we stop him from stealing more power."

"It's Luc," Bentley replied. "It's all about Luc! He should be able to set off his EMP ability near Adam and bring that thing to its knees."

"Then help me find Luc!" I screamed back. "Luc and Lacene are the only ones not here yet!"

Adam was almost free. My telekinetic box had widened some after his escape attempts, and I was nearing a point of exhaustion in using my powers that meant I would probably pass out soon, giving Adam carte blanche to rage against my friends.

As it turned out, Luc and Lacene hadn't even gone to a movie like the rest of the first watch crew. Instead, they'd gone to the Hollywood Hills looking to find the homes of the stars. And they'd turned their group radios off—more accurately, they'd never turned them on after arriving in LA, but the end result was still that they were not going to hear any radio messages and no one was going to find them while searching inside and around the Hollywood Walk of Fame.

As they strolled by the homes of the famous, they could see and feel the electricity in the air racing past them.

"Something's up," Lacene said, activating her telepathy to send me a message; if she had a general idea where I was, she could typically get a thought to me without issue. *Phillip, what's going on?*

Big fight. Bad guy. Need Luc. Where the hell have you been?

Lacene put her hand up to her earpiece.

"Holy crap, the radios!" Luc cried, making the same realization. They were a good mile or so from our location, and they were going to have to hoof it.

Luc punched the send button on his radio and started speed talking immediately. "Luc and Lacene, on our way."

"Get your butts here now!" I yelled. "Luc, we are counting on your EMP to shut this show down before it gets any bigger, do you understand?"

"We're on our way," he responded.

Right about then, Adam finally broke free of my grasp, brute-forcing the force field upward through timed jumps only to slide his fingers under the lower edge of my restraining walls, kicking off with his legs as leverage to pop open the trap.

Immediately he renewed his electricity-sucking activity, clearly more interested in that task than in fighting or subduing any of us attackers—for now, at least.

"How about this?" Patrick cackled with glee as he arrived with a cyclone of dirt from nearby Runyon Canyon Park.

"Perfect," came Penelope's voice, much more confident than normal. "I'll add the wrath of a steady rain and a thick fog!"

Everyone was soaked head to toe in mere seconds, such was the downpour Penelope had brought.

I could hear Adam start shorting out, loud sparks of electricity lashing out from all over his giant frame.

Pat's sandstorm and Penelope's fog had truly created a visibility problem. And it worked both ways. We no longer had eyes on the enemy.

Just then, Freddie reappeared with a small water tower—the kind that served a rich, exclusive community where city water was deemed too plebian.

Several stories tall, and running at full speed, Freddie's swing packed quite a wallop. But as he swung through the dust storm and rain storm and fog . . . he hit nothing, and thereby sent himself tumbling over and over into the air, crashing down a few blocks below Hollywood Boulevard, destroying several buildings in his wake.

"Where'd he go?" I asked. "Did he disappear? How did he disappear!"

"He did not," came the unmistakable voice of Adam from directly above as he pounced on me in a surprise attack. "He merely changed his approach."

It's not enough to be all powerful—this guy's learning sarcasm now too?

Adam landed on me like a tractor trailer, smacking my skull into the pavement and giving me a definite concussion. But Adam didn't care about my health; he cared only about his objective, and currently I stood in the way of him completing it, so I was the target. He'd learned enough from our two encounters to know that I was the leader of this group, and taking out your enemy's leader is solid *Art of War*–type battle strategy.

"Why do you resist, when you are so clearly outmatched?" Adam sounded as curious as he did menacing, like he genuinely struggled to compute our actions. His full weight continued pressing Emm and me into the sidewalk below.

"I could say the same thing to you, you oversized space heater," Freddie cried. He'd worked with Patrick to retrieve the water tower he'd mis-tossed earlier, and this time they had the element of surprise.

"Eat this," Patrick barked. Freddie's strength and size hit Adam with a bomb of water, shorting him out and sending sparks flying everywhere.

Right then—finally—Luc and Lacene arrived.

"Bonjour à tous, pardonnez notre retard," Lacene said just before Luc activated his EMP power.

An EMP is loud. It's like a reverse sucking jet engine of a noise, seemingly pulling at all the electricity in the nearby area before shifting and blowing it all back out—like a blackout bomb for anything that requires electronics.

Emmaline and I were still struggling to get up off the sidewalk, but Patrick could see fine what happened to Adam when the EMP went off. He ran. Technically he flew "like a bolt of lightning racing back up into the sky instead of falling down." Fast as light.

Adam had known what Luc's arrival meant, and he got the heck out of Dodge before it could incapacitate him.

"He's gone!" Patrick yelled.

Emergency sirens rang out, and in addition to cops and medical personnel, the Custodial Containment Force and their military robots would surely be here any minute.

"Everyone key in on me and prep for return home, ASAP," I barked. "Sherpa, come here!"

For now we'd saved one city from having its energy stolen by Adam, though maybe only for tonight. But we also confirmed that Adam wasn't some unbeatable supervillain. We learned that he could be fought, and fought by us.

I considered the whole thing a win, though a few under my command disagreed.

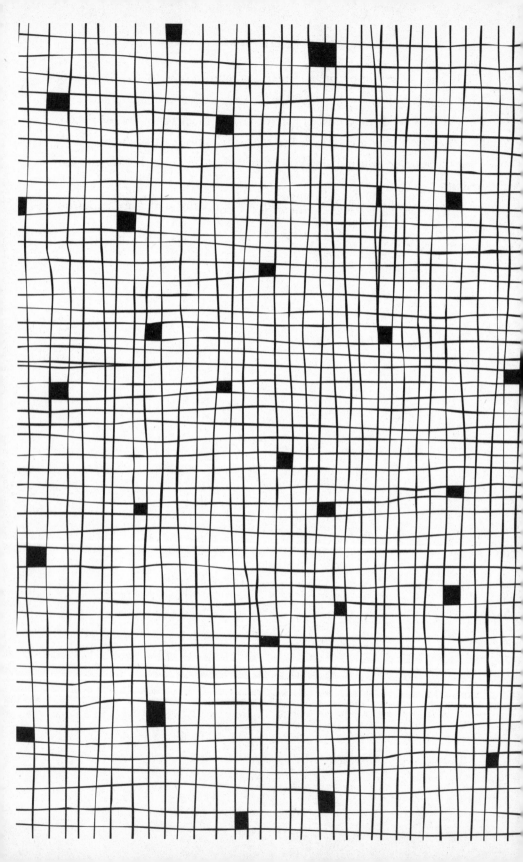

20

DEBRIEF

"So in order to stop a blackout, you caused a blackout?" Dad was pretty upset, and I couldn't say that he didn't have good reason to be.

"Strategically speaking," Bentley said, mistaking this for a classroom, "it's a fine tactic. Like wildfire fighters that burn a line of forest in order to stop an oncoming fire from burning farther and faster."

"Bentley," Dad started.

I thought I had an even stronger counterargument. "We blacked out, what, a hundred thousand homes and businesses?"

"Two hundred thousand," Dad corrected me.

"Two hundred, okay," I said. "But we stopped Adam from stealing electricity from ten million homes."

I could tell that Dad was upset, but most of his frustration wasn't with me as much as it was the circumstances and the repercussions.

I decided to seize the moment. "We worked well together as a team. We were creative. We did all the things you've ever preached at us to do."

"I know," he said. "I saw it on the news. The whole world saw it on the news. You guys picked one of the most heavily surveilled corners in all the city. Six different HD security cameras at nearby businesses—*six*—captured part or all of your showdown with this . . . what did you call him, Adam? Why did you call him Adam?"

"That's what he said his name was," Patrick said bluntly.

Dad sighed and took a couple deep breaths. "Okay, maybe I'm not mad at you. Maybe I'm just worried about you. Maybe I'm worried for myself because this is now going to be the first topic of conversation tomorrow at work, and being your father, I'll be in the spotlight."

"I'm sorry," I said. And I was. "I don't think we broke any of those rules, did we? The custodian rules?"

"You guys stole a private water tower from a gated community and damaged twelve structures."

"This is probably a bad time to tell you I promised my friend Nate an interview about the fight in LA," I said, figuring I might as well face all the parental backlash at once rather than spacing it out.

"You what!" he bellowed.

"He's a freelance journalist and wants to write about custodian issues. He gave me some pointers on my speeches, and in exchange I agreed to give him an interview after our next custodial event."

"You absolutely cannot give that interview," Dad said, sounding flustered.

"I promised," I said. "I gave him my word."

"If you give an interview about this to your friend, there's a chance it gets picked up on the newswire, and that will only complicate my job in defending your actions in Los Angeles and the damages you caused."

"Is there no consideration for Adam's part in those damages? Or what would have happened if we hadn't been there? They'd have lost all power— and not for a few hours but for days, just like Chicago and just like New York and just like London." I was on a roll. "The cost of doing something was far less than the cost of doing nothing."

"I agree with you," Dad quickly stated. "Not everyone on the board will, though. There are some hard-liners, as there are on most boards with any kind of political importance. I've told you for years I would never tell you not to hero, and I won't tell you that now. You are always free to be yourself, son, and I will support your decisions. Just . . . remember . . . your actions impact more people than just the ones present when you use your powers. There's a ripple effect. We all represent all custodians now."

"Does your board have to scrutinize every custodian event?" I said, shocked.

"Well, the ones that make the national news, we sure do!"

I sighed. "If you want us to pass off the pursuit of this guy to another custodian team, we can," I said, only for Patrick to smack my arm in response. "We're capable of dealing with this, though," I stated honestly.

"There's weird stuff going on all over the world, you guys," Dad said, sounding frustrated. "Most of the formal teams already have assignments that rank just as important or more important than the energy thief."

"Adam," Bentley corrected.

"Yes, Adam," Dad said through a forced smile. "Thank you, Bentley."

"What do they got out there worse than our energy thief? Is it giant alligators?" Patrick asked excitedly. "I bet it's giant alligators."

"You don't need to worry about the other stuff," Dad replied predictably. "You have enough on your plate." Generally details about other custodian assignments were on a need-to-know basis.

"I don't have anything on my plate right this second, but if I did I would eat it," Patrick replied jokingly. "Especially if it wasn't broccoli."

"Oh, pizza!" I said, joining Pat's attempt to turn the pep talk into a pizza party.

Dad relented straightaway. "Alright, alright, one of you guys call it in. I'm going to go take a shower."

I whipped my head in Patrick's direction, and he turned to look at me. The race for the phone was on. Patrick's biggest mistake was not going under the table in front of him. Instead, he moved—lightning quick, mind you—to stand and go around behind Bentley's chair. This was a longer path than necessary, so he arrived to a cradle on the wall that had no phone, just as it smacked into my hand back over at the table.

"Dang it!"

I laughed as I dialed. "I can't even remember the last time you beat me."

"I beat you plenty," Patrick countered. "I beat you three weeks ago, when that lady from the bank called."

"What? I wasn't even here for that." I was lying. I'd been there, and he'd beaten me, but I enjoyed tormenting him.

A voice on the end of the line interrupted my teasing. "Hello, Jack's Pizza."

⚡

"EMDR is different for everyone, Phillip," my therapist began. "The basic idea is to use rapidly repeating patterns of vibration or light to help rewrite how the brain processes traumatic memories."

"Vibration or light?" I asked. "Not both?" Part of this was me being curious, and part of it was me wasting time to delay the inevitable. I'm sure my therapist knew that.

"I think we'll start with vibration and sound for you," she said, as though I had any idea what that meant. "Headphones and a pair of handheld paddles. Rapid back and forth, then we'll slow it. But I'm getting ahead of myself. That's not important right now. The first thing we need to do before we start EMDR is talk about some of your most traumatic memories and see if we can find the very earliest one in your life."

"That sounds fun," I said sarcastically.

"Did you start coming to therapy for fun?" She had two ways she dealt with my snide remarks; she either ignored them and carried on or shot them right back in my face. I suppose it depended on what I needed most, or deserved.

"No," I replied, like a scolded schoolboy.

"One of the biggest drivers of your anxiety, Phillip," she said kindly, "is the sheer amount of trauma you've experienced in your young life. I believe this treatment will help cool the heat of that trauma and those memories and help lower your day-to-day baseline levels. But you've got to trust me."

"I do." I did.

"And this session may not be fun, and we may even take two or three sessions to lay out the specific memories that are most triggering for you. But it will be worth it when we're done, I promise you."

"I'm ready to try almost anything."

"Let's get started. What are some of the memories of traumatic events that haunt you the most?"

This felt like it was going to be easy as cake. "Henry's death. James's death. Donnie's . . . whatever, disappearance, I guess." I paused, finding myself emotional. "Mom."

"What about your mom?"

"Her death."

"What else?"

"I had to fight my dad—a couple times. And, you know, my grandfather tried to nuke the whole town."

"Go on."

"A lot of people died or got injured in that fight with my grandfather . . . Mr. Charles . . . so many students and teachers." She said nothing, which I understood to be a silent urge to continue. "That stuff I did when I was under the spell of that puppet-master lady. The video she played when she put me in prison."

"The video of the man using his powers after having a pain chip implanted?"

"Yes."

"Interesting."

"What's interesting?" I always seemed to be *interesting* to my therapist.

"That you mention that video—which you only heard the audio for—before you mention the trauma of ripping your own pain chip out of your hand with the raw force of your telekinesis. Something tells me that event, that action, was traumatic. Do you not agree?"

"I suppose it was traumatic. It hurt like hell, I can tell you that."

"Well physical pain isn't always connected to emotional pain, but in this instance I think it probably is. The decision you made, in the flash of a moment, to intentionally endure what you knew to be searing pain, in order to gain your freedom and use of your powers . . . well, I think that says a lot about your character, but it had to be hard to hurt yourself on purpose."

"I think it was hard for Henry too."

"Maybe. But that's not quite the same. He was literally saving the world."

"Yeah, I guess."

"I'm noticing a pattern here, early on, Phillip," she stated, with a tone that suggested she'd spotted something I had not. "Can you guess what it is?"

"Um," I thought, not really wanting to play games right now. "That a lot of people around me have died?"

"Okay," she allowed, understanding that my answer was not incorrect given how the question had been asked. "That's fair. But that's not what I meant." She took a deep breath, the way someone does when they know they want to word their next statement carefully. "I asked you about traumatic memories, and all the ones you've mentioned have been from a specific time in your life—the time since you'd received your powers . . . your life as a custodian."

"Isn't that when the trauma started?" I asked, blissfully unaware of how naïve I must have sounded. "I don't . . . I don't understand."

"Oh, Phillip. Those events are trauma, and we'll get to them, we will. But I'm trying to get deep into the root traumas from your younger days. The things that scarred you so much you might not even realize they were traumatic, but the events that set you up to fail later in life when your anxiety came calling. Henry's death, your mother's death—both would be traumatic on their own, but those events were made far worse for your mind because of the traumatic events that had come before them."

"You think there was trauma in my life before I got my powers?" I was still baffled.

"Are you kidding me?" she said with a scoff. "A blind child in public New York City schools, oldest of two boys, parents away all the time on missions—yes, I think there are trauma events in your early life, Phillip. And it's up to you and me to find them, talk them over, and reposition their importance in your emotional filing system."

"Alright." I didn't know what else to say. Whenever I wasn't sure what to say or if I didn't understand the question, I usually just said "alright."

"Let's talk about your childhood. You grew up in New York, right?"

"Yeah, we lived near Central Park. Close enough to walk but not right on the park like the high society types. Good schools. Mom and Dad were working as a custodial team, but we didn't know it at the time. We thought they had normal jobs and were just very busy."

"Do you remember any times when you felt lonely? Did you ever get lost or separated from your parents in a public place?"

There was a long pause as I realized she was right. I did have a memory like that. And I hadn't repressed it or forgotten it so much as I'd layered on top of it all the fresh, more recent memories that hurt. "Yes," I finally admitted.

"Tell me about that. Take your time."

"I got left at school once. I'm pretty sure it was an accident."

"Phillip, this is not about blame. We are not talking about your traumatic memories in order to find a villain. Plenty of traumatic pain is caused on accident, or by no one at all. Think about a tornado that hits a town and destroys people's homes. That would be traumatic, but it wouldn't be anyone's fault, would it?"

"No," I said, getting her point perfectly.

"Okay, so continue. How did you come to be left at school?"

"I'd been enrolled in an after-school program for disabled kids. I was about eight. It was supposed to give us extra time with a qualified teacher in the room, time to finish assignments or ask questions, free from the distractions of the bustling daily school activity. In the long run it turned into a glorified mandatory study hall, so I'm not even sure why I got so upset about getting left there."

"Try not to pause and reflect so much just now. Present-day Phillip will have time to comment on these memories down the road. Try to just describe what happened and how you felt."

"It was a new program, so it wasn't part of our family routine. But I was excited about it, because they were really selling it as a chance for me to stay up to speed with the rest of the kids in my classes despite my lack of vision. Now, usually I took the bus, and that was fine." I paused. "Actually, I hated the bus. I think there may be traumatic memories of riding the bus, so let's make sure we come back to that."

"Okay," she said, seeming to smile, probably because I was starting to remember more and more and embrace the process.

"Anyway, there aren't any buses an hour after school gets out, so I was going to need a ride. I had been on the subway before, but never by myself at this point. So I go into Mom and Dad's room that morning, and I hear the hair dryer going in their bathroom. And . . . honestly, I know you said to try not to comment in reflection, but . . . I really feel like part of this is on me, because I tried talking to Mom about an important detail while she was in the middle of getting ready and blow-drying her hair. If I'd waited a bit, or talked to her the night before . . ." I trailed off. "Anyway, I reminded her

I needed a ride after school at four. She nodded her head without turning from the mirror and said 'Okay, honey,' and I thought that was that. I'd come home with a note three weeks prior announcing the program, and I was sure she was already aware. I didn't even think I needed to remind her."

I could hear my therapist taking notes.

"And ultimately it turned out that I did need to remind her, and even though I did she still forgot. Or didn't hear me. Or both."

"So at four o'clock, she wasn't there?"

"Nope. And by the time I realized she wasn't coming—after thirty minutes waiting in the rain—I found the school had already been locked up and I couldn't get back in to stay dry or even use the phone."

"That sounds pretty scary."

"It was," I agreed. "I didn't have any money, so I couldn't take a cab or take the subway. I didn't have a beeper or a cell phone—I was eight! All I knew was that I had twelve blocks between myself and home, and no way to get there except to walk."

"Oh," I heard her exclaim softly, in a rare display of emotion.

"And I know the route just fine, because I have traveled it on the bus back and forth for years." It was amazing how quickly I changed from a cautious patient not sure he could remember older memories to a seasoned storyteller recalling every detail. "No umbrella, no windbreaker. And so I just walked. Just walked all the way home. It took more than a half hour. I tapped along in front of me with my cane. I listened for the crosswalk signal noises. I said 'pardon me' and 'excuse me.' But no one helped me. No one asked if I was lost or needed assistance. No one even noticed me at all. Twelve blocks I walked home, sopping wet, invisible to the world."

The therapist had stopped scribbling notes altogether now and sat silently, rapt with attention and waiting for the rest of the story.

"I finally get home, and the doorman won't let me on the elevator because I'm too wet and they'd just redone the elevator carpets, even though no one cares about the carpet in an elevator. Whatever. I climb all six flights to our apartment's floor, walk down the hall to our home in the corner, apartment 609, and find it locked and utterly void of human life."

"What?" She sounded shocked.

"Turns out my little brother, Patrick, who is sighted and not disabled in any way, had a part in his school play that night. He was barely a year younger than me but went to a different school, for reasons I never understood. They sent the blind kid to a public school—granted a fine school, but a public one—and they sent the able-bodied kid to a private school. Almost as though they had given up on me before I even had a chance to fail."

At this point, lost in the rediscovery of this memory, I nearly forgot I was in therapy.

"So Patrick, he stayed after school because the cast was doing last-minute rehearsals, and then they had to do makeup and costume changes to get ready for the big show. It was *The Little Mermaid*, and Patrick didn't even have a line in the play, he was just Background Fish Number Three. But Mom and Dad, they appreciated any excuse to go out to a nice dinner—a birthday, an anniversary, a promotion, or good grades. So they went out to eat at their favorite five-star restaurant before heading to the private school to watch their youngest son not act in the school play. Leaving me in the hallway outside my home, with no one inside to let me in and no key to open the door myself. I walked back down all six flights of stairs only for the doorman to tell me he wasn't allowed to let me into my own family's apartment without verbal permission from one of my parents, neither of whom were reachable at the moment. And I ended up spending a total of four hours shaking and dripping on the floor of our apartment building's hallway until finally my parents and brother returned."

I heard my therapist sigh.

"'And where have you been, young man?' my father asked. 'We assumed when you didn't come home from school that you'd gotten a ride with Stevie to your brother's play.' Stevie was a neighbor kid my age, who did go to school with me but would have had zero reason to ever go to my brother's play."

Now it was my turn to sigh. It was a long and somewhat painful sigh.

"I can't imagine how abandoned you must have felt in that moment, Phillip," she conceded. "I bet that series of events made you feel like no one cared about you and you would be on your own forever."

"Yeah," I agreed. "It did. I can't believe I had mostly forgotten that night."

"It's just one of many events we are going to uncover, remember, and then move on from," she replied warmly. "I think we've had enough progress for one day. Let's pick it up here next time."

21

INFORMATION

"So what do we do next?" Patrick asked. "We stopped him in LA, but there's no reason to think he won't strike again. He may even strike LA again!"

Most of our Ables mission crew ate lunch together on the weekdays in the Goodspeed University food court. Everyone but Emmaline and Penelope was at the table at the moment, and the topic of discussion was how to react and respond to the Los Angeles encounter.

"Is the camera Emmaline placed on the satellite still working?" I asked. "Can we see where he went after Los Angeles?"

Bentley sighed long and hard. "Unfortunately, that satellite was on the other side of the planet during the Los Angeles battle. So . . . while I picked up Adam's trail hours later when the satellite was back over North America, I have no idea where he went immediately after the event or within the seven hours after the event."

"Man," Patrick moaned. "We went through all that trouble to put a thermal camera on a satellite, and it's only useful half the time?"

"Emmaline went to most of the trouble," I corrected him. "But still, that sucks. Have you given any more thought to my idea about revisiting the abandoned base?"

"Some," Bentley allowed. "He's been there once in the last day, while he's also been to that spot in the Amazon three times in the same span, a spot where we all agreed we found nothing. I can only assume at this point that he knows we are trying to track his movements and is acting in ways that attempt to obfuscate our investigation."

"So we don't know anything?" I barked, mostly at the universe more than Bentley.

"Oh, we know plenty," Bentley countered. "We just don't currently have any actionable intelligence, is all."

"Tell me again . . . why can't your algorithm predict Adam's next target after Los Angeles?" Freddie asked Bentley.

"It's working on it," Bentley replied. "But when we interrupted the blackout attack on LA, we interrupted my algorithm's logic point. So now the thing can't decide if LA is still a target or not and can't settle on any next target as a result. It keeps giving me four cities, the same four cities, but always in a different order of importance—Cleveland, Nashville, San Francisco, and Atlanta. But the entire algorithm was based on weighted city importance, and I never wrote any code to compensate if one city's attack got interrupted by dweebs like us."

"So we have four possible spots to patrol. First problem," I barked out like a seasoned commander, "figure out which city to target. Second problem, how do we do better this time than we did in LA, assuming we do accurately predict the city and find Adam again?"

"What did we learn from last time?" Bentley asked.

"Well, I can hold him for a good minute or so," I said, referring to the air cage I'd employed outside the Chinese Theatre, "but not much longer."

"Okay, so next time we all attack together," Freddie said, "instead of the first person to spot him starting without the rest of us."

He had a good point, and I had acted rashly in Los Angeles. I decided to admit defeat here. "You're right. I acted too fast in LA. We should all be together the next time we move on Adam."

For a moment, it seemed I'd shocked the crew into silence.

Just then Emmaline and Penelope arrived with their lunch trays.

"Wow," Emm said, noticing the extreme quiet. "What's everyone not talking about?"

"Okay," I said, refocusing the discussion. "How do we search for Adam in four cities when we have only one teleporter and one speedster? Man, even for Patrick I think running from Boston to San Francisco would be a hike and a half."

"Maybe we just put Emmaline on standby," Bentley offered. "She stays neutral until we find a location, then she snaps to each other city to pick us all up and take us to the final destination."

"If you guys aren't standing exactly where I expect you to be standing, though," Emmaline said, "I can't zap from city to city so fast."

"Why only American cities?" I wondered aloud.

"Proximity to his hideout?" Freddie asked.

"He hit London though," I countered.

"Maybe it's the type of electricity he needs," Patrick suggested.

"Like, if he's hoarding electricity, I don't even understand why a city like Nashville or Cleveland would end up on his target list," I argued.

"Maybe he needs a specific amount of electricity?" Penelope offered. "So he's nearly filled his coffers but needs a little more . . . like a Nashville amount more, whereas an Atlanta portion would be too much?" Bentley was clearly rubbing off on her, as her ideas had gotten more and more inspired since they'd been dating.

"Then why are both cities on the list the algorithm spits out?" Freddie retorted. "We have two midsize cities and two large cities here."

"Is there no way to reduce our options from four to two?" I asked.

"It's actually five," Bentley admitted, "because a return to Los Angeles being possible is what throws the rest of the prediction algorithm out of whack."

"He's not going back to LA," I said with confidence.

"Okay," Bentley allowed, seeming surprised, "why do you say that?"

"Adam is a creature of efficiency. I'm not even sure he's human. Even when we confronted him in LA he still stuck to the blackout plan to suck in the electricity before attacking us. He's driven by priorities and odds." I felt like I was making sense, so I continued. "The odds would tell him to avoid LA—the only city where he's faced even a little resistance."

"Alright, great," Bentley allowed. "You've convinced me that LA isn't a target. How do I choose among the next four possible cities?"

"You just told us that your algorithm was struggling only because LA had become a fly in the ointment and thrown off the math. But if we use logic to remove Los Angeles as a possible target, can't we just go back to using your algorithm to find the next likely target? Tell your algorithm that LA got hit and is off the table. What city does it spit out?"

I heard the familiar sound of Bentley furiously mashing keystrokes as he coded on the fly. Eventually his code spat out some information. "Nashville," he finally revealed.

I was a bit disappointed, if only because I was hoping to visit a foreign city, which seemed like a silly, selfish thing. But I trusted Bentley's math and even had a little bit of firsthand experience in Nashville, though I tried to forget most of it, so I was ready to go. "Nashville! Really? Okay, Nashville! Let's do this!"

"It won't be for another few days," Bentley reminded me and everyone else. "Remember, Adam is seemingly on a prime number–based schedule, and the next prime number is five. It's only been one day since the LA event. I'm just saying. I like that energy, but let's save it for the right day."

It was time for our third speech of the semester. We'd all started out with the terrifying impromptu speeches, followed next by the stylish persuasive speech, wherein we'd all taken hard stances on mildly divisive political issues in order to sound impassioned while speaking.

The third style of speech we were to learn was the informational. And I'd decided to lessen my school workload by choosing a topic I knew a lot about: service dogs.

Which made this an unofficial Bring Your Dog to University Day.

"This is Sherpa," I began my speech.

A chorus of oohs and aahs came from the audience before me. And indeed, Sherpa was an adorable dog, even before you learned how smart she was. She was a cutie, for sure.

"She is my mental health service dog, and right now she is on duty. The service dog vest, which reads 'Please don't pet me while I'm working,' is her uniform. When Sherpa is wearing this vest, she knows she is on the job, and her job is to help me cope with stressful and anxiety-inducing real-world events. Whenever I remove the vest, Sherpa understands that she is off duty and can feel free to run and play and seek out pets like any normal dog."

The class was in love with Sherpa already, I could tell from their verbal reactions to her introduction. And having the class fall in love with my visual aid was 100 percent part of my strategy to get a good grade on this speech.

"Because of her training, Sherpa is able to help me in a variety of ways. She can detect signs of my anxiety before my own brain can even detect them and help drag me out of anxious situations. Sherpa can fetch medication or water whenever I have an anxiety attack. She's trained to bring me a phone or find another able-bodied person nearby to help, she knows how to apply pressure in her kneading paws to help relieve stress, and she's capable of recognizing environmental anxiety triggers and leading me out of such surroundings."

I was feeling good about my speech, but I wanted to make sure I mentioned some important stuff for low-income families. "Service dogs and training facilities can cost a lot of money. Most recipients of service dogs for mental health rely on scholarships or extended payment plans. So donations are always welcome to help fund the boarding and training of these dogs."

I felt really good about the speech after I'd wrapped up and headed back to my seat, Sherpa in tow. I'd covered the points I wanted to stress, and I hadn't passed out during the speech; this was a vast improvement on previous efforts.

I sat back down in my seat and closed my eyes, saying a quick prayer to the college gods that Dr. G graded based on overall improvement rather than a hard scale based on speech quality.

These days, nighttime proved just as interesting as daytime.

That night I had another nightmare.

I shouldn't have been surprised, as they'd become fairly regular lately, especially as I encountered more and more new troubling events and situations.

In tonight's dream, I was on a log flume ride at an amusement park. The water was carrying us along.

"Where are we going?" I called into the night air.

In the log with me were Luc, Lacene, Greta, and Echo—all the most recent Ables members.

The path of the flume ride was predetermined by the track. The end of the ride predetermined by the nature of the ride—a steep fall into a body of water that would splash everyone on board. I'd ridden this flume many times and thought I knew it by heart.

Just as the log tilted to begin its descent, I heard Greta say, "Here we go." She seemed to be comforting Echo. "I always forget the twists and turns, but the end result is always the same."

But the log tilted itself up for a sudden moment, only to then tilt down and keep tilting until we were literally staring down a straight drop.

Gravity took over and we dropped, collectively screaming as we fell to what we all assumed was a certain death.

Greta turned to me, mid death fall, and said cheerily, "I always wanted to know how I would die. Thanks for helping me understand." Then she shook my hand, with ferocious strength, and saluted me, before reclining in her seat.

The log then crashed into a massive pool of water, and the nightmare turned into one of pure survival as I struggled to swim my way up and out of the megadeep body of water.

I swam for what seemed like hours and finally reached the surface. But when I came out of the water, it was no longer a pool at the end of a flume ride; it was a bathtub, and my mother was standing there shaking her head at me saying, "Not clean enough. Scrub harder."

22

NASHVILLE

Nashville is a booming city in Middle Tennessee that serves as the state's capital and the official birthplace and home of country music.

Residents would tell you the city is much more than country music, with a thriving rock scene, fine arts fans galore, and a rich mix of cultures.

It's also the city where my friend James died, mostly due to my own selfishness and shortsightedness, but that's a thought better held for my therapy sessions. The point is, being back in Nashville reminded me of James immensely.

The memories of that battle with the dragon-form custodian was seared into my brain, and I got a second wave of guilt when Henry popped up in those memories.

For reasons that made no sense to me, James's family believed in burying people in the place in which they died. I was a little hazy on the origins of that tradition, but the end result was that I got to visit James's grave while we were here.

Most of the group hung back, because they had joined us after James had passed.

Only Patrick, Bentley, Freddie, and I had been close to James, and the four of us gathered around the marker in somber silence. Several minutes passed as each of us remembered James in our own way. Finally I was compelled to speak.

"James," I began. It was part prayer, part poem, part therapy. "I miss you, buddy." I heard a couple grunts of agreement around me. "I miss your optimism. I didn't always love it when you were alive, and it sometimes made me crazy, but I miss it now. I need it." More verbal agreement from the other three. "It's not your fault you died. I think it's mine, but others disagree, but the point is it's not your fault. You did nothing but go about the business of saving lives as best you could. And I took it for granted. Just like I took Henry for granted." At some point I forgot there were three other Ables with me and subconsciously leaned into the confession. "I'm not going to do that ever again. I'm not going to forget you, and I'm not going to take any other custodian or human for granted again."

Everyone either verbalized their agreement or stayed silent. An impromptu moment of silence, if you will.

Finally I asked, "Did anyone bring any flowers?"

Whoosh. Patrick had just gone off to—

Whoosh.

"Here," Patrick said, holding up what I assumed was a nice arrangement of flowers.

I reached out to grab them, asking, "Do I even want to know where these came from?"

"Not any of the other graves," he offered sheepishly.

"Did you at least leave some money behind?" I asked urgently.

"Of course," he scoffed. "I'm not a barbarian."

Bentley had given Patrick a fresh new set of shoes designed to not only hold up better than average sneakers under all the extra work he tended to give shoes, but also to help him go even faster. I was personally a little terrified about it.

Everyone was getting new toys from Bentley's workshop lately. Freddie had a new inhaler that was more efficient than the previous design and didn't result in so much wasted medicine.

And Greta had a visor. Typically her "light beam" appeared to come from her face, and Bentley thought the visor could allow her to focus the beam to higher and tighter configurations, or even cast a wider light to cover more ground.

"You got any computerized eyeballs cooking in that workshop?" I'd asked.

"Ha ha, no," he'd laughed.

I'd been joking, of course. But I'd also been secretly hoping he'd say yes.

⚡

The geographical-electrical center of Nashville was, for once, basically the actual center of the city. There were plenty of energy pulses outside of downtown that threatened to pull the geographical-electrical center southeast or northwest, but they were so evenly spaced around the city itself that the GE center ended up being Second Avenue and Broadway.

One block from the river, the amphitheater, and a few hundred yards from a professional football stadium.

I remembered being inside that stadium on the field itself, lashing out at James. Recklessly tossing that beast over the Cumberland River into those buildings.

It felt like yesterday, even though it had been around seven years.

"Let's make a plan this time before we go charging into battle willy-nilly," Bentley said, echoing the sentiments of most of the team. Clearly I'd messed up in LA when I tried to do everything myself at first. I was actually glad to let the entire group make the plan this time out.

"We know water was bothersome to him," Penelope stated before continuing her thought, "and we are really close to a river."

We were sitting together at a picnic table in a park along the river. The temperature was fine, but the breeze made things a bit chilly.

"Agreed," I said. "How can we incorporate the river?"

"We could push him in," Patrick offered.

"Well," I couldn't resist the older brother jab, "*some* of us could push him in." The implication being that Patrick himself couldn't do it alone.

"I'll push him in," Freddie offered, not getting the joke but making a sincere offer.

"Well . . ." I said, pausing for a small group of tourists to walk by. "What's the objective? Do we want to stop him from stealing the city's energy? Or take him prisoner? Or kill him? The objective drives the plan, I think."

"I agree," Bentley said. "And we aren't here to kill anyone or anything."

"Total agreement," I replied.

Bentley continued. "So the primary objective has to be stopping the theft of the electricity, but we can't ignore future cities he might target, and so capture has to be part of the mission, otherwise we're just goofing around here and not taking our jobs seriously."

"I agree. Subdue then capture. That's the mission." I paused and remembered we were a team. "What do you guys think?"

I heard affirmative noises all around.

"Alright, how about Penelope swoops in first with a rapid fog. And just when Adam's realizing his vision is depleted, Patrick and Freddie move in from slightly different angles. Pat gets there first, because he's a million times faster than Freddie—even three-story-tall Freddie—so he binds the legs of Adam with good old-fashioned rope."

Everyone nodded or grunted their understanding so far.

"What if his energy just burns through the ropes?" Patrick asked.

"Well," I sputtered, "then run and grab a bunch of rocks from the river or a construction site and build a little wall to trip him."

"I like that a lot better," he said.

"Awesome. Then," I continued, "Freddie rushes in with the linebacker tackle, knocking Adam into the river."

"Once in the river," Bentley took over the narration duties, "Phillip and Emmaline will pin him underwater with a force field, which will last anywhere from thirty to sixty seconds."

"Luc," I barked, "that's thirty to sixty seconds that you have to plunge into the river and set off your EMP powers."

"How do we know I won't do long-term damage knocking out you or Emmaline or any other Ables in that water?" Luc asked.

"We ran all kinds of simulations on the computer," Bentley answered, "and most suggested there would be no issue. But there's no guarantee or anything."

"I don't care about the simulations," I blurted out. "I care about stopping these blackouts. Whatever this energy is being stolen for, it's going to be bad, and I'd just as soon never find out what it is because I did such a diligent job checking everything now." I breathed in deeply. "If I have to sacrifice myself in order to make him immobile underwater so one of you can knock him out of commission . . . that's a sacrifice I'm willing to make."

"It doesn't have to come to that," Patrick replied.

"It's not going to be an issue," Bentley reiterated. "The odds are incredibly slim. You'd be more likely to win the lottery."

"My aunt won the lottery," Greta said excitedly, not realizing the context at first.

"Big help," Bentley sniped.

"Lacene, I know most of us aren't sure what Adam is, human or otherwise, but I think it's time for you to try and get inside his mind and see what's there."

"I'll try my best," she agreed.

"That's all I'm asking." Then, to the group, "Everyone understand the plan?"

"Guess we just hang back," Greta mentioned, meaning she and Echo.

I started to reply, but she cut me off.

"No, it's okay. I get it. We don't want Echo trying to touch this guy to use her powers, and I'm not even sure I could blind him with my powers anyway."

"Stay close, and stay safe. Things are bound to go wrong, as they tend to do, and we may need you."

"You got it."

"Alright, everyone. Let's get in position. We may have to wait a while before he shows."

We waited.

And waited.

And eventually people were spilling out of bars and restaurants buzzing about the latest blackout attack—in Mexico City.

When we told Bentley's algorithm that Los Angeles had been hit, we'd lied to it. But it had added the appropriate amount of energy to Adam's stores. So at that point the algorithm didn't think Adam needed very much more power, and spat out a smaller, midsized city like Nashville.

In reality, Adam had been chased off in LA and had acquired very little new energy that night. Therefore, he was in need of much more electricity than a city like Nashville could offer. He needed something bigger than LA; he needed Mexico City. And now he had taken it.

It was such a simple mistake I wasn't sure how we'd made it. It had been me who had suggested we remove LA from the algorithm's target possibilities list, but I hadn't recognized the ramifications of such an action.

Bentley must have been too flustered after so much tinkering with the code.

We did pop down to Mexico City once we learned the news and did what we could to help.

Freddie grew large and propped up an apartment building that threatened to fall over, keeping it upright while the EMTs and cops evacuated all the residents. A bus had crashed into the first floor and taken out one of the main support beams.

Lacene was a godsend, putting out mental feelers for anyone who might have stopped yelling for help but was still mentally hoping for it. She found several folks we were able to rescue from elevators and wrecked cars. Sherpa went around sniffing out people and animals that needed some kind of attention or rescue.

There were a few fires here and there, and Penelope created tiny localized rainstorms to put most of them out. The others were put out by Patrick doing his rapid-back-and-forth thing with buckets of water from a nearby lake.

Emmaline teleported around some of the taller buildings, explaining the blackout to some folks and helping others get to the ground floor if they needed medical care.

Greta finally had another chance to shine—literally. She gleefully powered up her abilities as a high-powered flashlight, locked into the harness Bentley had built for Emm and me, and I used my powers to lift us up into the air, a makeshift sun providing light for rescuers and citizens alike.

As I hovered there in the air—basically being an elevator for Greta to get up high—I realized that while we'd missed out on a confrontation with Adam, we probably ended up doing more heroic things with our time anyway.

And I smiled.

23

DOUBLE DATE

Every now and then, Emmaline and I would go out with Bentley and Penelope. I don't think Bentley enjoyed the experience very much, as he was always a bit quiet and seemed caught between friend-Bentley and boyfriend-Bentley.

But Emm and Penelope had become close, and it was their friendship that drove the double dates.

Tonight the ladies had chosen the destination, and we were in a fancy steak house in Boston. Remember, teleporting is a fantastic quality to look for in a significant other—I cannot stress this enough. Dinner in Boston? Sure, here we go, and now we're here.

Bentley was his usual quiet self, really only piping up when spoken to directly.

The gals were talking about the latest album from Sarah Swan, arguably the biggest pop star on the planet. The previous record she'd released wasn't very good, they'd decided, as it tried too hard to stretch into new musical genres. The brand-new one, though, was a delightful return to her twangy pop stylings.

I considered weighing in. I could have; I had opinions about Miss Swan's music. But it was more fun listening to them. Truth be told, like Bentley, I didn't mind a little quiet time, even if it came in a public setting.

The waiter came, and we all made our selections. And eventually talk turned to work.

"I thought it was nice doing regular kind of rescue stuff," Penelope said. "Sometimes the more action-based custodian work is stressful."

I was about to agree with her when Bentley muttered, "I can't believe I still haven't found him."

I paused before responding. "Well, I think you're being too hard on yourself."

"He's always doing that," Penelope said. "He's way too hard on himself."

"Alright, alright," he said, a bit on edge. "I don't want to talk about it."

"Well, maybe we need a break," Emmaline suggested, trying to lighten the mood. "It's not too long until Christmas."

"Sure," I said. "But how many other cities are going to lose power between now and then? Or worse, what if no other cities lose power, because he's got all he needs?"

"I was just trying to . . ." she sighed.

"I'm sorry," I said right away. "I didn't mean to be a downer. I'm just . . . I'm concerned about this stuff. I don't think I want to take a break."

"We're kind of taking a break right now," Bentley said. "Even if it's for only an hour or two, we're sitting here in Boston in a restaurant waiting for food that will probably taste good. And maybe we enjoy each other's company. But there's not one of us here whose time wouldn't be better spent working right now as opposed to being here."

It was a bit to take in, for us and for the waiter, who'd arrived with our waters just in time for Bentley's rant. He took off as quick as he could without saying a word.

I was pretty sure I didn't want to be the next person at the table to speak, so I lowered my head a bit and took a deep breath.

"Are you saying," Penelope said, a little louder than I'd have preferred, "you'd rather spend this time in your workshop than with your friends? With me?"

"It's not about what I want," Bentley said. "The work is more important than me or my wants. Every hour not spent working is wasted. I'm sorry, yes, even this dinner." He suddenly stood and pushed his chair in. "In fact,

I'm going to leave. Sorry, Phillip. Sorry, Emmaline. Pen, do you want to stay here or come with me?"

Flustered, Penelope simply stood up, apologized, and the two of them left in a hurry.

Emm and I sat in stunned silence for a good thirty seconds.

"So I guess we're getting the bill," I finally said.

We both laughed, and the tension was broken.

"Man, I have never seen anything like that," she said.

"I've seen him get mad and huffy like that, but never with Penelope— only with me, or Henry, or about his dad."

"What do you think is going on?"

"I don't know. Maybe he's just super stressed about finding Adam. Or maybe he's upset that we missed last time out."

"So strange," she said.

I assumed Bentley was going to use a custodian teleporting service to get home to Freepoint. Or he could hire a private jet if he wanted. The way he'd stormed out, I honestly didn't care how he got home.

"Now there's a guy I'd like to see get some therapy," I added, only partly joking.

"Oh," she almost cheered, "speaking of therapy! You were supposed to tell me about the new treatment thing you were doing. How was it?"

"Wow, straight to the heavy stuff. No fair," I said to no use.

"I don't need to know any details, that's not what I mean. That's for you alone. I just thought it was a new process or something, and I wanted to know how it worked and what you thought of it."

"Yeah, I know," I agreed. "Apparently before you start the new treatment process, you have to talk out all your traumatic memories."

"That sounds fun," she sneered.

"That's what I said! Anyway, the treatment is about taking power away from traumatic memories, but before you can start you have to know what those memories are. Apparently quite of few of mine have been repressed."

"Ugh. That sounds like the opposite of a good time, though. That sounds upsetting."

"It was. I had this whole recalled memory of being left at school to walk home alone in the rain. I'd forgotten all about that. And it does hurt to talk about some of it, but I guess that's the point, or so I'm told. It'll be painful at first, but the idea is that, if the treatment works, those memories won't ever be quite that painful for me again."

She squeezed my arm. "Well I like the sound of that."

"Me too."

The food arrived, and we turned it into one of the most memorable meals of our lives. We laughed and sampled all the food our two friends were no longer around to eat. We played a casual game where we started sharing things with each other that we thought the other didn't know. She learned that I was deathly afraid of spiders, and I learned that she used to have a pet spider. She learned that I had been thinking about writing a book, and I learned that, in addition to French, she'd been learning sign language so she could talk to Echo.

It was a great date and only affirmed our mutual affection. She zapped us back home, outside my house, and we promised to talk if either of us heard from Bentley or Penelope.

Ooph!

Then she was gone.

⚡

Nate Weller's story about the Los Angeles event had indeed been picked up by the newswire and became an international piece of journalism. Nate himself was relatively famous overnight, at least in journalism circles.

No one had ever landed an exclusive interview with an active custodian, which I suppose is part of why Dad was upset that I'd done the interview; we weren't supposed to do them. I was just honoring my commitment to a friend.

He was over at the Sallinger house to interview me again, this time about Mexico City. I'd warned him there wasn't any energy monster or battling in this story. "I want to report the custodian news, whatever that news may be," he'd said in a cheery tone.

I was even happier to grant this interview, as it would showcase my team as true heroes. The action of the fight in Los Angeles was probably a more exciting read, but heroism came in all shapes and sizes. Rescuing people in danger after a massive blackout is heroism.

One of my favorite things about Nate was his optimism. It felt like a quality I used to have. He was so positive about being a journalist, and he spoke of the news as a holy thing. And he'd done well enough in our speech class, I could imagine a future where he was on television reading or reporting the news. He was one of those go-getters that you kind of knew was going to make it somewhere.

We talked about Mexico City, and when we finished he put away his notebook and tape recorder and we talked for another hour about life stuff. He was seeing a new girl, Amber. He was having trouble picking a topic for his motivational speech—the final speech each of us had to give in class. I told him a bit about my crazy dreams, and my blackouts.

We were in the middle of agreeing about how annoying it is to have a little brother when Emmaline popped directly into the living room.

Ooph!

Of course, at this point, I knew her teleportation sound; I knew her smell. "Well, hello there, Emm," I said, pretending this was a regular occurrence, or trying to.

"Holy crap," Nate said, sounding out each syllable slowly, stunned to witness an unexpected teleporter arrival.

"We have a problem," Emm stated, her tone making it clear things were urgent.

"What's up?"

"Where do you live?" The direction of her voice told me Emmaline was speaking to Nate.

"What?" Nate was still in shock.

"Where do you live?" Her tone was exactly the same as the first time she'd asked it.

"Goodspeed, Langdon Dorm, third floor," he said, a little scared.

Ooph!

I sighed, pretending this wasn't cool and hilarious.

Ooph!

She'd just zapped Nate home with her abilities so that she could talk to me in private. She could be blunt; she preferred the term *direct*.

"Bentley broke up with Penelope."

"What!"

"She showed up at my house, bawling her eyes out. Said they fought after they got home from the restaurant."

"Oh man."

"She said he kept accusing her of talking to him like his father used to, putting him down and belittling him. She said she was just trying to help him stay upright during a moment where he stumbled. Bentley said it didn't matter anymore anyway, he'd found him, and he wasn't going to be hanging around here anymore."

"Found him?" I said, mostly to myself. "Adam?"

"His dad, maybe?" Emm thought out loud. "I don't know."

And that was the moment. That's the exact moment everything clicked for me. That's the moment I knew where we had to go and what we had to do. And I wasn't looking forward to any of it.

24

THE FORTRESS

I messaged the entire team first thing in the morning, telling them I had new information and there was an urgent mission. I instructed everyone to report to Bentley's house in an hour, which they did inside of an hour, dressed in warm clothes as instructed. Everyone except Penelope, I should say. A few of us knew why, but we didn't make it public knowledge.

I was the last to show up, a little bit on purpose. I wanted to make the jump as quickly as possible, and with as little discussion as possible.

"What's going on?" Bentley asked, naturally.

"What's with all the secrecy?" Patrick asked, faking it.

"There's no time. This is urgent. If you trust me, let's get hands in here. If you want to stay behind, that's fine too."

Silently, and one by one, everyone's hand made it into the center or on the shoulder of someone inside the circle.

"Let's go," I said to Emmaline.

As before, I felt something faint tugging at my coat just at the point of the jump.

Ooph!

Nate had stowed away again on a mission. I wanted to tear him apart right away, but the situation didn't allow for it. And I didn't want to call attention to him right away in a place where he could potentially get hurt or even become a target.

"What?" Freddie asked, a little annoyed that the big secret mission was a return to a place we'd already been. Specifically, we were back in the abandoned military bunker in the wilderness of Canada, which at this point in the year was a frightening 4 degrees Fahrenheit. The wind whipped in through the hole in the cave's sidewall, making it seem even colder than it already was.

"I don't get it," Patrick said. "Didn't we already come here?"

"We did," I said. "We came here, and we found Adam here."

The group murmured a bit.

Sherpa just stood at my feet patiently.

"It's so cold," Greta whined. In her defense, it was wicked cold.

I just continued. "Do you remember how he dropped just the smallest bits of information about himself and then zapped us all back home, knocking unconscious the two who could get us back up here quickly?"

More affirmative grunting.

"What kind of villain sends you directly to the ER?" I asked rhetorically before just carrying on. "Why not just knock everyone unconscious?"

Among the mumbling, this time someone actually spoke. It was Greta. "You're saying maybe he's not evil?"

"Think about it," I confirmed. "He knocked out only the two Ables he needed to in order to escape. He sent us to the emergency room instead of, like, literally anywhere else where medical help wouldn't have been instantly available. And when we confronted him in Los Angeles, he didn't attack. He just went for the electricity and tried to escape our makeshift force field prison. Does that sound like evil to you?"

"So what are you saying?" Patrick asked, probably on behalf of everyone. "That he's good?"

"Maybe he's good. Maybe he's just not bad. Or maybe he just *thinks* he's good. Remember, he mentioned a master. Someone's giving this guy orders. Someone's calling the shots and telling him what to do."

"But if someone's telling him what to do, and his actions are sort of kind," Freddie wondered, "then isn't that master also acting in kindness, by telling Adam to send us to the ER instead of some terrible other location."

"I agree with that," I said. "I think whoever is controlling Adam has good inside them and believes they are acting with good intentions."

Just then I heard a wave of electronic sounds, in a computerized choral pattern—a sigh from the just-arrived Adam.

Sherpa growled a bit until I tapped her on the head.

"Why have you returned?" the electronic giant insisted. He hummed and snapped with a raging energy surging inside his body. It seemed clear to me that, despite science, this dude was holding all the stolen energy from the past few weeks inside his person.

"Before you take all that"—I gestured toward him, waving both hands to indicate the energy stored inside him—"and use it for your ultimate purpose, I think we deserve a few answers."

"You deserve nothing," Adam replied.

"Are you human?" I asked, getting more direct. "Or are you some kind of robot?"

"I am something more." The air crackled with electricity when he spoke.

"More," I repeated. "More. Change of subject," I declared quickly. "What are you going to do with all that energy you're carrying around?" I was mostly acting, playing the part of a guy who didn't already know most of the answers even while he was asking the questions.

"It's time for you to leave. I will make you leave if I have to," he threatened.

"I don't think you will, actually," I said with confidence. "Not this time."

The rest of the group went mostly silent, sensing that I knew where I was going, but also kind of nervous about where it would lead.

"You see," I declared, "it's too close. Too close to the moment of truth, the hour of action. The penultimate prime number of days since the last blackout."

I thought it was pretty telling that Adam hadn't said anything in the last fifteen seconds. There was one other telling voice that remained silent.

"I think tonight is a big night—the night your job is over and your master puts you to work." I stepped forward twice. "In fact, I think your master won't let you kill us or electro-teleport us anywhere because he wants us to be here for the big reveal. He probably even has a whole speech planned."

I paused for effect, even though he already knew that I knew.

"Don't you, Bentley?"

⚡

I have to stop here and go back. Back to when Emmaline told me of Bentley and Penelope's breakup, and specifically what he'd said—that he'd found "him." And I, with my narrow focus, assumed he meant Adam, whom we'd been hunting. But Emm had wondered in the moment if Bentley had been talking about his father, and that was the key. Once I considered the mere possibility that Bentley was more interested in finding his father than he was in finding Adam, it all made perfect sense.

The lightning flash in his secret lab that day had probably been Adam electro-teleporting Bentley from the base back to his home.

The strange absences were times he spent at the secret base or on the secret invention.

The breakup with his fiancée was probably motivated by his intent to attack his father, even at the cost of his own life. Several years ago, Bentley's dad, Jurrious Crittendon, had been revealed as a mole for the toxic members of the US Government who had tried to put all custodians in internment camps. He'd escaped capture in the fallout of the fight on the National Mall and had been in hiding ever since.

Bentley had long harbored resentment for his father, and I had always assumed it was related to verbal or physical abuse of some kind. And after the battle in DC, he'd withdrawn considerably. I had assumed at the time that he was blaming me for Henry's death, but in hindsight, I think he felt shame about his father's actions—and eventually he vowed to make amends.

After Henry's death, things had gotten worse and worse between us. Then Bentley disappeared for over a month. When he returned, I sought him out and got direct with him, asking if he was mad at me. He said he had been but he was over it now and things would go back to normal soon.

And they did. In hindsight, I think he just realized he needed to be better at subterfuge and hiding his anger.

After Emm had whisked Nate home and told me about the breakup, my mental light bulb went off. We sent Echo a message and were able to meet up with her privately.

Echo, as you might remember, was a kinesthetic. She could touch items and glean information from them about their history, even flashes of video-like memories—and it worked for people and for inanimate objects.

Knowing Emmaline could manage a bit of sign language, the three of us teleported into Bentley's lab inside the Crittendon mansion.

After we arrived, there was a good pause.

"She said she feels guilty spying on Bentley." Emmaline was translating Echo's sign language.

"Me too," I agreed.

I heard Emm's hands and arms move as she signed back to Echo.

"We need to head to that secret lab," I said. I was familiar enough with the room by now to know I was pointing in the right direction.

The girls walked over there first, and Sherpa led me in following them.

Emmaline opened the door. Inside, she would later tell me, was a full secondary lab. The walls were lined with inventions, gadgets, and other miscellaneous parts.

"Find something on a shelf and take hold of it," I said, which Emm translated to Echo via sign language.

Ultimately Echo chose a snow globe. Inside the snow globe was a miniature version of the town of Freepoint. A lady downtown made them and sold them at the local flea market.

Before I could object to the snow globe choice as unhelpful, Echo saw some surprising and awful things and dropped the trinket out of sheer shock.

For nearly a minute I could hear the fabric movements as Echo signed rapidly to Emmaline. It was maddening waiting for the translation, especially knowing Emmaline was still learning and might not know all the signs Echo was making.

"She says it's Bentley," Emm finally said with the weight of a thousand exhales.

"What?" I knew whose lab we were in, so I wasn't sure what I was being told.

"Phillip, it's Bentley. He is definitely the one controlling Adam." Emmaline sounded like a newscaster reporting on a disaster, relaying information out of duty but feeling sad about it.

Now it was my turn to go quiet for a long time and frustrate those around me. I'd known it. I'd suspected it. That's why we were here. But it still felt like a sock in the gut.

A few hours later, one hour before the message to meet up at Bentley's, we met up with everyone except Bentley at my house to give them the basics.

"I believe he is making one of two pipe-dream machines he's always talked about. I believe he wants to use the machine to somehow 'fix'"—I made air quotes around the word *fix*—"his father's crimes. One is a time machine. Bentley has always talked about wanting to invent a time machine. And it sounds nuts to think about it being real, but so does an eight-foot energy creature sucking up entire cities' worth of electricity, so . . ."

No one spoke up, so I kept going.

"The other machine he might be building—the one I think is most likely—is a custodian-finding machine. Basically a device that scans the globe and uses trace custodial DNA traits and other factors to find any and all custodians all around the world."

"Holy, crap, it's like a Cerberus!" Freddie exclaimed.

"What?" Patrick asked.

"In the X-Men, the bald guy has a machine that lets him find other mutants—a Cerberus!" Freddie couldn't fathom why he was even being questioned about this.

"It's Cerebro," Luc corrected. "Professor X's machine is called Cerebro. Cerberus is, like, a mythical demon dog, I think."

There was some giggling, which seemed appropriate.

"The point is," I declared, ending the silliness, "Bentley seems hell-bent on using the energy inside Adam to fuel a machine he believes will help him find and kill his father. And it's up to us to stop it."

25

INSULT TO INJURY

"Don't you, Bentley?" I said, revealing my secret, though it was truly only a secret to Bentley that I knew he was Adam's master. The rest of the Ables gang had already been briefed.

There were gasps from the group as I said his name, though they were mostly acting. For now, we weren't ready to reveal to Bentley that everyone here knew he was the real target.

But Bentley wasted no time stepping out from among the group several feet, stopping between us and Adam.

He took two huge breaths and finally exhaled long and loud. "I have probably always underestimated how clever you are, Phillip," he began. He was essentially confirming my theory, but the room went quiet to allow him time to speak.

I merely crossed my arms, awaiting his twisted logic.

"This was going to be an incredible reveal," he said with a laugh, "and you totally ruined it! But I can still give most of the speech I prepared."

I snorted in a morbid laugh. "Sure. Let's get it over with."

"I told you," he suddenly roared, erasing all humor from his tone and sounding as angry as anyone had ever sounded, "two years ago, that I was going to find him, no matter what it took!" His voice echoed throughout the remaining portion of the cave.

"I thought you were just being emotional," I shouted. "I didn't think you were serious!"

"Why?" he shot back. "Because you had so many memories of me and my dad having fun times together?"

"No," I replied. "Because I didn't think you were capable of murder."

"Murder?" His tone was taunting. "Murder? What you call murder I call a sentence for crimes committed against humanity. Have you forgotten how many human and custodian lives he's personally been responsible for ending!"

"I have not forg—"

He cut me off. "Over three hundred twenty-five custodian deaths are linked directly to information he gave to our enemies. When you factor in the laws he influenced, the leads he gave the feds, and the sellout to that puppet-master woman in DC, he's negatively impacted over ten thousand lives of custodians and human-support families."

"Does that mean he needs to die?"

"Justice doesn't always look fair."

Adam crackled with power, silently standing behind Bentley like a pet on a leash.

"What the hell is that supposed to mean?" I spat. "You're mad as hell at Daddy, and you're going to take it out in a violent way rather than seeking your own peace." I kept going. I was on a roll. "And however good his death might make you feel today, it will only further delay the peace you deserve to feel about that relationship."

"My father is the greatest blight on this Earth in the last two hundred years," Bentley shouted, "and I will happily wipe him out, regardless of consequences, to keep him from ever hurting anyone else again *and* to punish him for his wrongdoings in life."

"Why don't you at least end the charade of this broken-down bunker," I cracked, letting Bentley know I was also aware of his hologram technology that was keeping this base from appearing operational.

"Ha," he laughed ominously. "Sure."

The fictional walls and facades digitally turned to nothing, and all the Ables but me were finally able to see that this was a still-functional base, with an entire subfloor basement base currently housing the machine in question.

"It actually *is* a Cerberus," Freddie whispered.

"In any other situation," I began, "I'd be impressed with you, Bentley. You've built all this, you've managed to keep it secret for years, and you've broken a technology barrier—so you say—that many thought unbreakable." I meant it too.

"Thanks," he said, sensing my honesty.

"But all this to get back at your dad?" I asked. "And you never once tried going to therapy or talking to someone about anxiety and PTSD? You've stolen so much power you've negatively affected millions of lives, just so you can tell your dad off? How did you make that work, morally?"

"Oh," he replied, laughing, "I left morals behind a while ago. Morals are relative. What you think is immoral may, in fact, be moral to me."

"Maybe it's time we stop the chitchat and get to the heart of the matter," I said sharply.

"Sure," he said, a smile in his voice. "I'm ready as hell to get to the heart of the matter. Let's get rid of some of the spectators, though," he said. I heard the clicking of a button.

And then all hell broke loose among the Ables crew.

A sudden shock zapped Emmaline out of the harness I was wearing, and she fell straight to the floor. Simultaneously, Patrick's ankles popped and Greta's visor crackled, and they both fell to the ground unconscious. Freddie's inhaler started hopping around in his pocket, and Luc's headband zapped loudly as well.

And just like that, my entire team was out of commission except for me, Echo, and Lacene.

Sherpa started barking at Bentley, now fully aware he was no longer our friend. "Stay, easy," I told her.

We had picked up the clues and guessed that Bentley was the real villain, but somehow I'd never given any thought to the new inventions he'd been handing out to team members.

What a simple and obvious oversight, I thought, scolding myself.

And now most of the team was wiped out in a single action, sabotaged by devices intended to help them save more lives. There was a wicked irony in Bentley using custodian-enhancement devices as Trojan horses to bring those same heroes down.

"What did you do, Bentley?" I gasped.

"They'll all be fine," he cackled. "Should all be fine. Merely passed out temporarily," he suggested. "Just took out all the friends you had that could actually stop Adam or defeat my ultimate plan."

I heard Lacene as she kneeled beside her twin brother, searching for signs of life, and Echo tending to Greta as best she could.

And that left only unconscious Ables . . . and me.

"All I have to do is turn this on," he teased. "And I'll know where my father is."

"Sure," I replied. "But you'll use all that energy, and you'll have no more Adam, no one to protect you once you plug that energy into your machine."

"Why are you so opposed to him facing justice?" he bellowed.

"I'm not. I'm opposed to him facing your justice, because you are too biased to be legally fair, and even the worst villains deserve to be treated fairly by our laws."

"That's the worst thing about fairness—the comfort it offers to even the most evil among us."

"Look," I stated, hoping to draw this conversation to a close, "neither of us is running for office, so we can both stop talking like politicians and just find a compromise."

"I don't have to compromise with you!" he screamed. "I have all the power! I hold all the cards!"

Right then Echo reached Adam. Unbeknownst to me, she had maneuvered over to his position unnoticed while Bentley and I bickered about things. And while she was mute due to the accident, she wasn't blind. And her power was touch-related.

Lacene was the only other conscious Ables member, and she finally stood and shook off the cobwebs in time to see Echo do something stupid. "Echo, no!"

"What?!" I yelled out.

"Echo grabbed Adam's left ankle!" she shouted back.

"Echo, tap your feet!" I yelled, realizing I could take advantage of this moment if I could get to Echo quickly.

"Sherpa, stay!" I pulled out my clicker and used it against Echo's tapping feet to levitate over to her location in just three seconds.

And as I grabbed Echo's ankle, and she held Adam's ankle, her powers flowed through to me, and the information she could obtain by touching an object also became information readily available to me. Echo became a conduit, as Adam's memories passed through her to my mind seamlessly.

Most of the rest of my account of Adam's memories came to me rapidly, sporadically, and with plenty of gaps. This shouldn't be taken as a full account of his life. And yet, after seeing it . . . maybe you wouldn't want to see the rest of his life.

The first flash was Adam as an elementary school student. Already taller than his classmates, he was scolded for being too good at basketball, and even given a time-out in the corner after recess because of it.

Adam's parents then died when Adam was ten. They were killed in a boating accident, and Adam was sent to foster care.

His first set of foster parents had eleven children. Four were their own biological children, the rest were fosters. On Adam's first day, his pockets were emptied—the contents given to the foster parents—and he was beaten up for his shoes.

The second foster home Adam lived in was a lot more loving on the surface, and for the first week or so Adam even felt a small sense of peace. But then the strange photographer started coming around taking family portraits that started creepy and only got worse.

Adam was much taller than his peers, and he was growing rapidly. But while he towered over his peers, he cowered from them emotionally, always aware that he stood out in a crowd and people were talking about him.

He escaped the second foster home and managed to hitchhike across three states before being picked up by the Missouri state police.

Once the troopers had verified his identity, Adam was put in his third foster home. The foster parents were in it only for the money, and the living conditions were below the bare minimum. There were cages. There were chains. Beatings instead of hugs; cuts instead of bedtime stories.

This was the place where Adam finally disappeared into his own mind, behind a shield of quiet subservience.

Adam's fourth set of foster parents locked him in a cage and fed him white bread and bologna for two years.

His next set of foster parents tried to sell his blood samples on the black market. And the sixth set tried to get Adam to sell drugs for them at school.

By the time he was seventeen years old, Adam had been in seven different foster home environments. That's when he ended up part of a Crittendon Foundation experiment trying to take foster kids stuck in the system and match them more rapidly with new foster parents. The new foster parents had undergone training and vetting to ensure they were caring and could also provide a good environment.

Adam and Bentley had met at one of the Crittendon Foundation picnics. Neither of them wanted to be there, and both of them hated their parents. The friendship was born over mutual boredom but hardened as they bonded over mutual anger.

One night, Adam got so angry talking about his foster parents, he briefly started glowing orange, and his voice wavered like a garbled digital recording. Adam was of custodian decent, but his parents had died before he'd come of age so he'd had no one to tell him. Adam had a power; he could store and release enormous amounts of energy.

Suddenly there were shots of training, as Bentley did for Adam what he'd done for Henry and me, helping him learn how to focus and use his abilities. As he mentored the brand-new superhero, Bentley became a sort of father figure to Adam, a guide in this strange new world, a sensei.

And finally Bentley had a way to build a machine he'd dreamed of for years.

The point is . . . Adam was human. He was freakishly tall without being outside the realm of possibility. And he'd been bounced around and abused by the foster care system so much that he'd taken his frustration and annoyance and hardened them into a stoic wall of protection.

He'd been swayed easily by Bentley's offer to "pay back the parents who have wronged us" motif. Heck, Bentley was like a priest to Adam eventually.

I let go of Echo as she let go of Adam, and I found myself to be in the middle of a primal scream. So much information, so many horrible memories, had rushed into my head all at once, which my vocal chords had decided to treat the way they treated pain.

THE DEVICE

"What have you done?"

"Oh, come on!" Bentley shouted back at me. "You get some memories from Echo's touch thing and suddenly you understand him?"

"Do you even have any idea what he's been through?" I spat. I walked slowly back toward Lacene and Sherpa, keeping a good twenty feet between Bentley and myself.

"Of course!" He sounded like he was bragging. "Why do you think I chose him!"

As we argued, forces beyond my control went into effect.

Most of my Ables teammates were out of commission, zapped by Bentley's nefarious Trojan horse inventions.

He wanted to leave me blind with little to no help when we faced off. He wanted me to feel alone.

Little did Bentley know, I always felt alone. It didn't scare me; it motivated me. The more he pushed me into a corner, the more I was ready to lash out.

"I don't have all day," Bentley sighed. "I've been waiting for this moment for years. I don't want to delay things by bickering with you. Conversations with you always end up in the same place anyway, you being right."

"So what? I'm just supposed to let you fire up your machine and stand by doing nothing?"

"I hope you won't stand," he replied.

Lacene, having found a pulse for Luc, was paying more attention to the environment now. *Phillip*, she told me silently, *he's got a gun*.

"So, what, Bent? You gonna shoot a blind guy?"

"Yeah," he said. And then he shot me.

I felt the impact in my right shoulder, but I didn't immediately feel pain. I felt warmth.

"Lacene!" Bentley yelled.

I slumped to my knees and then fell to the floor.

Sherpa barked violently at Bentley but was overwhelmed by her first duty, which was not revenge on my shooter, but looking after me, especially in times when I'd fallen to the ground. She whimpered as she nosed around me, smelling and looking for clues to my condition.

Bentley continued scolding Lacene. "You ruined another of my surprises! You guys are ruining all my surprises!"

"You shot me," I seethed. In all my many adventures, this was actually the first time I'd ever been shot. I was not a fan.

"Relax," Bentley snarled as I heard him start walking away. "You'll be fine. I'm not a killer, Phillip. I'm not a villain. I've been trying to tell you— I'm the hero." A few steps later, he said, "Let's go, Adam. It's time. It's finally time."

The floor of the facility was glass, so Lacene and Echo were able to watch Bentley and Adam walk down the stairs to the basement lab. They'd both come to my position, and Echo was trying to tend to my bullet wound, while Lacene told me about what she could see in the lab below.

The machine had two parts: one was meant to house Adam and all his raging energy, and the other was a smaller compartment for Bentley. Between the two sections was a gap about five feet across. I'd seen flashes of the same machine in the memories Echo had pulled out of Adam. I knew the energy would shoot from one compartment to the other completely over the air. At the edge of the smaller section was a filter that redirected the energy in thin little rivers all throughout, dispersing it.

Inside the smaller chamber was a computer, which Bentley could use to narrow his search for any particular custodian on the planet. He intended to seek only one, his father. We couldn't let him do it.

"Adam is climbing into the thing," Lacene said. I could hear her voice change directions as she glanced back at her brother midsentence. She was a good sister. "Bentley's closing the lid. He's turning the machine on."

I heard the dog turn her head and make a grunting noise, but it was too late.

Then there was a huge commotion behind us as what turned out to be a massive squad of CCF robots appeared.

"Wait, don't shoot!"

Nate!

I'd forgotten all about the fact that Nate had stowed away with us again. But before I could process and do or say anything in response to the situation, one of those meatheads fired. It was a robot soldier that fired, to be sure, but a human being at some nearby base was controlling it, and that's the one who pulled the trigger.

It didn't matter that it was a rubber bullet, because this one hit Nate straight in the eye and went directly into his brain, killing him almost instantly.

I heard his body hit the floor with a sickening thud.

"Nooooooooo!" I screamed.

"Cease fire, cease fire, stand down!" Most CCF squads were robotic remote-controlled soldiers, but they tended to have a human field commander, and this one was telling his soldiers to stand down.

Suddenly Bentley was back from downstairs. "General, General, what's going on?" he shouted. "Why are you shooting? Why are you here? We said tomorrow for delivery."

"You know this guy?" I asked.

I could hear Lacene sobbing behind me.

"Shut up," Bentley told me as he walked by my position on the floor. "General Rayburn. To what do I owe the pleasure, sir?"

"We're here to take delivery on the device."

"But you're early," Bentley declared. "I haven't even tested it yet."

"You tested it last night, son."

Bentley stammered.

"We may have needed your big brain to build the device, but we're plenty technologically advanced enough to spy on your progress while you do it. You didn't think we were going to give you all that money and not keep an eye on things, did you?"

"I don't even care about the money," Bentley shouted.

"He's got a hostage!" I heard from behind us. In a moment of panic, Bentley had grabbed the nearest potential hostage for leverage, and I knew immediately it had to be Echo.

"Everyone just back off or I'll shoot her! Now you can have the machine, like we planned, after I use it first."

"Don't do this, Bentley," I begged. "You're better than this."

"No, Phillip," he corrected me, "*you're* better than this. Me? I've never been all that good." By the sound of his voice, he was backing away from everyone, probably toward the staircase back down to the basement laboratory.

"You can't let him use that machine," I said, turning toward this General Rayburn, not knowing exactly where he was.

"Stay out of it, hero." His voice was filled with contempt. I'd heard stories about the people who ran the CCF and the soldiers in its employ . . . stories that they truly did hate the very existence of custodians. That they viewed us as mutations. They weren't even mad just about us doing hero stuff, they were angry we were sharing the same air. This guy sounded like one of those types.

I just sighed. *Fine, I'll do it myself.*

I'll help, Lacene thought into my mind. *What can I do?*

Talk to Echo, I replied. I hadn't had a full conversation entirely in thought in a very long time, not since Henry. *She's touching Bentley right now. He's forgotten all about her abilities. I don't know how targeted her abilities can be, but see if she can find out how to break this machine. I know there's a way, and I know Bentley knows what it is.*

But she can't talk.

No, but she can think, right?

Ah, gotcha. I'm on it, Lacene agreed.

There was a good pause of several seconds.

"Alright, men, let's move forward slowly." The general was going to pursue Bentley, and I'm not sure I had much confidence he cared about what happened to Echo.

She says just disrupt the energy flow once it's turned on, with something big. That should kill the machine.

Isn't it on already? The machine? Do you see the energy flowing between the two pods?

Yeah. It's on. Bentley's getting into the smaller pod now, and Echo is running back up the stairs. The soldiers are moving in faster now.

Faintly, I heard Emmaline groan and realized she might be about to wake up. And that gave me an idea.

I heard the soldiers start to jog and decided to quit caring about quiet thought communication and just use words. "Gather everyone. Get Greta and Patrick, drag everyone close enough so they can all be touching. Hand to foot, head to head, I don't care."

"Echo's here," Lacene announced. "Echo, help me move all our friends so they're all touching."

I was relieved Bentley had let Echo go, and even more relieved the CCF soldier robots had decided to ignore her.

"Sherpa," I said, pointing in the direction of where I knew some of my unconscious friends lay on the floor. "Drag." And off she went. Sherpa knew a ton of verbal commands, and she loved nothing more than to follow them.

I pulled myself to my knees and slid Emmaline over to me by pulling her shoe. I made sure her hand was touching Patrick's hand. "We have to get them all out of here," I told Lacene and Echo, "in case that machine explodes."

The plan I had in mind would definitely explode the machine.

"The soldiers are starting down the stairs," Lacene told me. "How long does that machine take to work?"

"I don't know," I replied. "How are we looking here?"

"We're all set. Everyone is touching someone in the chain."

"Alright, you two join as well."

"We're not going to leave you here alone!"

"Lacene," I said firmly but warmly, "you are. I am not going to give you an order. I don't need to. You need to make sure everyone here wakes up okay, and if I succeed then there's going to be an explosion here that could kill or hurt you. You have to go. You have to."

"Okay," she finally agreed.

"Sherpa," I said, grabbing her with my left arm, while my right arm hung limp from the bullet wound. "You have to go too."

I heard her whimper. She understood that I was telling her to go even though I wasn't personally out of danger yet. In any other situation it would have been a sweet and tender moment.

"You make sure Emmaline gets home safe, okay, girl?" I kissed her head, and she licked my neck.

I handed the leash to Lacene. "Ready?"

"No," she said honestly. Then she gathered herself and answered again. "Yes."

I had remembered the incident back in Chicago when Emmaline woke up while we were falling. That's how I'd learned of her safe place, and how reflexively she sometimes sent herself there. I was counting on it happening again.

I leaned over to Emmaline, who was on her back. I didn't touch her, and I stayed far enough above her to avoid her sitting up quickly and hitting me or anything like that. And then I started screaming.

"Emmaline, oh my god, we're all gonna die! Ahhhhhhhhhhh!"

Within a second, I heard a noise that made me very happy.

Ooph!

If I was correct, I had just saved my entire team's lives by exploiting my girlfriend's safe place teleporting situation, sending them all into her bedroom back in her parents' house in Freepoint.

I stood to my feet.

This is going to hurt very much, I thought.

I levitated myself off the glass floor, used my hearing to pinpoint the open section of floor on the far wall where the stairs went down, and took a quick deep breath before hurling myself right at the wall, full speed. I tried to lead with my good shoulder, and definitely dislocated it when I smacked into the far wall.

I broke a few ribs and one of my ankles while tumbling after throwing myself down the stairs to the lower lab.

I could hear the robot soldiers shouting, though I was in too much pain to know if they were yelling at me or at Bentley.

I knew the rough layout of the machine from Lacene's description, and there was no mistaking the over-the-air energy transfer between the two pods, as it roared like a rocket.

"Stop!" I heard the general yell.

"Stop!" I heard Bentley yell; he must have popped the lid, seeing what I was about to do.

I just smiled. For a single moment I felt none of the pain from my recent injuries. I felt none of the emotional pain of my past traumatic experiences.

I realized it had been weeks since my last blackout. All I felt was peace— peace that can come only when one is fully confident they are making the right decision, I peace I had rarely felt myself.

And then I remembered Henry. He'd smiled too, there at the end. I hadn't understood it then, nor for the four years since, but now I finally understood that smile.

The energy beams were so strong, I barely had to use my telekinesis to fly into them. They pulled and tugged gently at everything in the room. As I let go, I thought about Emmaline. I thought about Patrick and Dad. And I hoped they would forgive me.

And then as I merged with the beams . . . everything went black.

27

THE LIGHT

After ages of blackness, there was a speck of light. A dot. But it was bright, and it felt important. So I moved toward it.

Going into the light is something people joke about with near-death experiences. But I didn't think this was a near-death experience at all. I thought this was post death.

Regardless, light seemed more hospitable than darkness.

As I walked, the light grew larger. Soon something that was once so far away was nearly upon me.

I entered the light to find a seemingly endless field of golden-yellow flowers. The sky was bright blue, free of clouds, and a cool breeze rolled over the hills.

Over one hill came strolling a tall gentleman. He waved like an old friend, and in what seemed like only a handful of steps he was upon me.

Instantly I knew.

"Adam?"

He nodded. He looked like a normal human, though extremely tall, and no longer had any of his energy look or robotic vocalizations.

"What is this place?"

"Not sure, to be honest," he replied. "I mean, these are the fields next to my grandfather's house. I used to run among these flowers with other kids in the neighborhood—this was back before Mom and Dad died. It was my favorite spot in the entire world."

I looked around and took in the view, not really concerned with the fact that I was seeing right now, as though I had eyes. *Maybe in the afterlife everybody has eyes*, I thought.

"It's not real, of course," Adam said, gesturing to the flowers around us. "This isn't my grandfather's actual field. None of this is real. And you're here, and I'm not all energized, and you can see. No, I figure this is some kind of temporary holding cell between life and death."

"Great," I said. "Why did I get lumped into your version of purgatory instead of my own?"

"What would your happy place be?" He seemed genuinely curious.

"A cornfield in my hometown maybe. Maybe the ocean."

"The ocean is nice," Adam said with a smile. Then he put his hand on my shoulder. "I should never have let Bentley use me like that. I had it rough—there's no lying about that, and I wouldn't dare try to fix—but that doesn't excuse . . . um . . . what I did back there at the lab, and in all those cities."

"I don't blame you, Adam." And it was true, I didn't blame him. Life had dealt him eight garbage hands in a row, and then he met Bentley. And Bentley had been hell-bent on a selfish quest for revenge.

"I probably deserve to die," he said plainly, with the same tone one would use to describe what color their shoes were.

"Why do you say that?"

"I have done too many evil things."

"You were influenced," I argued. "You were manipulated."

"But I'm not all bad," he stated.

"Certainly not," I agreed.

"I think they allowed me to have this place, and these few moments in it, to right a couple of the wrongs. I did enough right, maybe, that I get to take a couple things back."

I didn't know what he meant. For all I knew this was a dream, born out of my own subconscious.

"So I will save you. I will keep you from death."

"How?" I asked. "Why?"

"You have shown selflessness. You threw yourself into the machine to stop it. Only someone pure would do that."

I had a good laugh at the idea of myself as someone pure. My self-esteem had never been good enough to let me think of myself as pure.

"You and Bentley. You both deserve to live."

"Bentley?" I didn't exactly want to be wishing anyone would die, but I didn't understand Adam's willingness to show kindness to someone who had tormented him. "He used you. He used you for his own revenge."

"You saw my memories, yes?" Adam asked.

"I did. It was . . . it was hard to watch. I wish I hadn't seen any of it. You endured so much at the hands of ruthless adults."

"You see more good in me than evil, because you look beyond my recent actions to see the pain that inspired and ultimately led to them."

"Yes."

"Then do the same for Bentley," he grinned. "For if you could touch him and see his memories, you would find far more terrible things to regret having seen, and you would understand."

I knew. I'd always known Bentley's father had been mean and uncaring. I never dreamed it could have been like what I'd watched Adam go through as a child, or even worse.

"I think time is up," Adam said. "I can feel myself being called back over that hill." He shook my hand and walked away toward the hill he'd arrived on.

"Will I ever see you again?" I called.

He stopped and turned back. "What an odd question for a blind person to ask." Then he laughed, waved, and walked on up and over the hill.

The explosion of Bentley's machine had obliterated the lab and everything in it, including the machine itself, all the CCF robot fighters, the late General Rayburn, and the body of one Nate Weller. And Adam, I assumed.

It was so bright and large an explosion that the astronauts on the space station had been the first to report it to any authority or governing body.

Only two had made it out alive.

Bentley and I both awoke in the emergency room of Freepoint Hospital. We'd arrived just seconds after the explosion, and within moments, we were being treated.

Adam had used his considerable energy to carve out a small pocket of time. He'd used it to reflect on his life and his actions, and to explain to me why he was sparing the two of us. I came to believe he had hoped to start Bentley and I down the road to reconciliation, but I wasn't sure how that was ever going to be a possibility.

I was in the hospital for a few weeks. The bullet had been easy enough to remove, the wound easily stitched back together.

But the many broken bones kept me laid up for quite a while. I had visitors every day, including all the Ables gang, my family, and Sherpa of course.

For the first few nights, Bentley came to visit me late at night when he thought I was asleep. He never came into the room, standing only in the doorway. And he never said a word. I knew it was him because of the sound of his arm braces and the unique gait it created for him.

I was too angry to want to speak with him, so I just let the beeping machines fill the silence until he would leave.

After a few days, Bentley was released. And by the time I myself got out of the hospital, Bentley was gone. His mother said he'd transferred his personal savings, said an abrupt goodbye, and left without telling anyone where he was going.

If he and I were ever going to make peace, it wasn't going to be anytime soon.

Emmaline had come on release day to walk me home. She'd brought Sherpa, who would surely have been offended if she hadn't been included on the walk.

"Penelope hasn't heard from him either. I think it's pretty clear he wants to disappear," she said.

"That's fine with me. I have no interest in seeing him."

"Maybe you will one day." She squeezed my hand.

"Hey," I said abruptly. "You like me for me, right? Not for my powers or because some custodians think I'm famous, but just . . . for me, right?"

"Of course," she replied. "I'm kind of offended you would even ask me something like that, after all we've been through together."

"I just wanted to make sure."

I'd done a lot of thinking in that hospital bed. I was going to make some major changes in my life, and I wanted Emmaline to be one of the unchanging things, one of the constants.

28

FINALS

It was time to present my motivational speech. I'd been shaky enough all semester that my grade almost certainly hinged on this final speech. And I had gone wildly off book for this one.

Dr. G always said that a good speech started from a place of authentic emotions or opinions. I could only hope she meant it.

"Why I'm Quitting the Custodian Life—and Why You Should Too." It was common practice to name your speech's title before launching into the thing.

There were some gasps, as I'd expected. After all, I was relatively famous within the custodian community, mostly from my involvement in some of the most famous events of the last eight years.

I was also standing in a university designed for custodian heroes, giving a speech to a room full of custodian heroes.

"Custodian work is noble and good. It is necessary in this world. But it doesn't have to be done by you. In fact, I will go on to make an argument that your best life you could possibly live is one that eschews the hero stuff altogether and focuses on family and friendships."

A few whispers came from the class, probably in the vein of "I can't believe he's saying this" or "where is he going with this?"

"Make no mistake," I continued, "any one of you who chooses, after listening to my speech, to still be a hero custodian will have my respect and support. This speech is not about disparaging the custodian lifestyle. It's about being realistic about it."

I didn't have note cards like most speakers in class, because note cards for a blind person are super unhelpful. I lobbied Dr. G all semester that I should get a half letter grade bump just for having to memorize all my speeches whereas my fellow students did not. The professor did not agree.

The point is, I was free to move my hands about while I spoke, and though I hadn't rehearsed anything, I felt my arms getting into the message of the speech, gesturing to emphasize my points.

"Before I became a custodian, I never had panic attacks. I never had PTSD, depression, or anxiety. And while I cannot draw a direct line from hero work to my mental health struggles, there's no question it's connected."

I rattled off the many events that had been traumatic for me, the battles and deaths, the losses and defeats. Then I rattled off the mental and physical toll these events had taken on me, from sleeping outside and blackouts to therapy and medication for stress. "The doctors got so desperate they wanted to start nanite brain therapy to try and confuse my brain into being less anxious."

Whatever grade I ultimately received, this was undoubtedly my most honest and impassioned speech. I could tell I had everyone's attention, as normal room noise—pencils being tapped, coughing, etc.—had dropped dramatically.

I powered through the meat of the speech, rattling off example after example of well-intentioned young custodians I'd known who had either ended up injured, dead, or corrupted entirely into evil and selfish lifestyles.

"Being a hero, more often than not, breaks you in some fundamental way. It changes you. It becomes part of your identity."

I stopped a moment, briefly emotional at my own words. I found composure and continued.

"It changed me into a person with massive mental health issues. Or were those issues there all along and being a custodian only intensified and sped up the arrival and onset of those conditions? Maybe." I paused for effect. "Or maybe not."

I was ready to wrap it up with my big finish.

"A lot of what I've said here today is speculation, far from true science or fact. But here's what I do know. Since I made the decision to stop active custodial work, I haven't had a single panic attack. I haven't had a single blackout. I haven't been depressed. My service dog has fewer chances to do her job helping me with anxiety, so she's started gaining weight. My insomnia is gone—I slept ten hours straight last night, and I haven't done that since I was in grade school."

They were rapt with attention, even if they still didn't understand why I, of all people, would be giving a speech railing against being a hero.

"Now, if you take all that information and put it into context . . . why would I ever go back into hero work again? I've literally never been this free of pain and worry and sadness. I'm happy again. Maybe some of us, though born with super abilities to hero parents, simply aren't cut out to be custodians, at least not without facing consequences. Lord knows my nineteen years of life have been full of compromises, and I'm kind of tired of making them.

"I am free to be me, and my abilities don't mean I have to live the stress-filled life of a superhero. You're just as free as me. Do you feel pressure? Do you lose sleep over your actions in the field? You don't have to. It doesn't have to be that way. Maybe you can find the heroism in the everyday things that I'm focusing on lately—volunteering, charitable donations, carrying groceries for the elderly, or just bringing a smile to the faces of the people you encounter along the way.

"But as for me . . . I'm hanging it up. This is my retirement speech. I'm no longer anyone's superhero." I paused but only a half second before finishing. "And I've never been happier."

As I walked back to my desk, the rest of the class applauded, as was the polite custom in a speech class, but I could tell the applause was more awkward and tentative than usual. It was as though they either didn't actually like the speech or weren't sure if they were allowed to.

I walked by the desk Nate always used to sit in, feeling his absence acutely. Usually he'd sneak me a sly high five or secret handshake as I went by.

I'd been unable to talk to Nate's family, because the lawyers wouldn't let me. Nate's parents were blaming me specifically, and the custodian government in general, for their son's death, even though every witness stated he'd latched on to my coat and teleported to his eventual death of his own free will.

Dad was pretty sure we were going to win the case, but until it all shook out legally I wasn't allowed to have contact with them. Even though all I wanted to do was apologize—actually I could see how apologizing would look bad for our case, and I'm sure that's why I was forbidden. But the whole thing struck me as just one more reason to step away from the custodian life and the custodian society.

No one else was going to die on my watch.

$$\frac{\textit{4}}{}$$

"And how do you feel today, Phillip?" my therapist asked.

"I feel great," I said, no guile or trickery to my words at all. For the first time in ages, I actually felt completely free of anxiety and depression.

"No anxiety?"

"None right now," I replied truthfully.

"Nothing to fear or worry about?"

"Not anymore," I replied. "I've given up the ghost. What will be will be."

"You're saying you've given up the hero life? You've retired to a life of an average American citizen?"

"That's right, yes."

"So do you even get the calls for help from the other Ables still out there fighting the fight?"

"Sure, from time to time I get contacted," I admitted. "But it's typically something I have no interest in or a realm I have no sway over, so . . ."

My therapist was cautious, but she seemed to see enough change in my demeanor to think I wasn't crazy. "And what about Emmaline? How does she feel about your walking away from the custodian life?"

"She's been super supportive," I answered right away. "She's still active with the Ables and doing hero stuff, but she understands and respects the decision I made, and why I made it. She's not tempting me to get back into the life or trying to change my mind. She said she likes me for who I am, not for what I do."

"And how about your dad?" she asked. "Your brother?"

"They've both been supportive. Dad's just happy I'm not having blackouts anymore. I think Patrick wishes I would come back, but he'll be fine."

"I'll be honest, Phillip," she said. "I do see improvement. I see a happier, less anxious person before me. I just caution you against making absolute decisions or taking absolute stances on anything right now. You're nineteen years old, almost twenty. So you've given up being a hero and you feel a lot better already—that's amazing. I love hearing that. But you will find that as you age, you change. And as you change, you revisit things."

There's nothing a nineteen-year-old hates hearing more than the fact that when they grow up they will understand things better. Adults might as well yell "nanny nanny boo boo" at them. Still, she'd been a great help to me, and I vowed to give her opinion its full weight.

"What if you and Emmaline get married?"

I laughed in self-defense.

"You've been dating for several years, and you care a great deal about each other. Is marriage so far out of the realm of possibility?"

"I mean . . ."

"Just stay with me. This is a hypothetical situation, okay?"

"Fine," I agreed.

"If you and Emmaline were to get married and have children, those children would have a 99 percent chance of having custodian genes— superpowers." She paused, perhaps for drama's sake. "Would you give them the same speech your father gave you? Would you let them be heroes or try to keep them from going down that path?"

"That's a lot of ifs," I reminded her. "But I guess Emm and I would have to cross that bridge when we came to it."

"You're fine if your future kids go into the hero business? You're okay with that even though you've rejected it?"

"Sure," I muttered. "There are days I want to get back in the game . . . make better use of my abilities than getting a drink from the fridge without having to get out of my chair." I sighed. "But look at what it turned me into. Look how much of a mess I was when you met me. You yourself said you could see massive mental health improvement in me."

"It's true," she agreed. "I just want to make sure you find balance. There is a path that allows you to still be a hero from time to time, but not going so full bore that you're never thinking of anything else. Moderation." She cleared her throat, and I could tell the session was about to be wrapped up. "But my job here is to shepherd and safeguard your mental health, and I am definitely pleased with your progress and improvement in that area."

"It feels good to feel good again. For a while there, it just felt like I was always waiting, worrying, planning."

"Well, we're out of time," she said with a smile in her voice.

My therapist always left the schedule up to me. If times were tougher and I wanted to meet weekly, it was my call. If I was doing okay, maybe I'd schedule the next appointment for two weeks out, or three. But I loved that she let me have some say in the frequency of appointments. It helped invest me in my own treatment.

I knew what her next line was going to be. And I'd honestly not yet thought about what my response would be. I knew I felt good. I was set for a little bit, on an upward trend. But at least some portion of that confidence was phony; I knew myself well enough to know how capable I was at lying to myself.

Finally, and long before I'd found any answers, she said the line she always said to end a session. "So when would you like to get together again?"

A smile crept across my face as I realized I was in complete control of the answer.

⚡

That night, I had no nightmares at all.

THE END.

ACKNOWLEDGMENTS

I continue to rely on the support of so many as I write this series of books, including but not limited to: the great people at Turner Publishing, my friends at MadeIn, my CinemaSins family, my business partner Chris, my editor, artist Callie Lawson, my friends, my family, my early readers (Quade, Jess, Jonathan, Isaac, Christopher, Barrett), and most importantly my wife—who pushed me to write these stories down. A final thanks to the Ables readers, for your time and attention, and for being willing to take the journey.